"You must know all the homeowners, Chief," I said. "You've been out here a long time."

"Over sixty years. Me and my wife built this house with our own four hands. Almost lost it in the hurricane of thirty-eight. That was something, I can tell you. In the summer of thirty-nine they had to rebuild this whole town."

"Except this house."

"Right." He took a drink of his lemonade and stared off. "And I remember the other disaster, the biggest fire they ever had on Fire Island, right here in Blue Harbor. Nothing left of that house except the chimney."

"Was anyone hurt?"

"They were lucky. Lost everything except their lives. Nothin' left to pack up. They got on the ferry and never came back."

"You have quite a memory," I said.

"Yup. I remember everything. I remember folks that came and went, folks that stayed for thirty, forty years, little babies that grew up here and then built themselves for their own families. And I know where all the bodies are buried. . . ."

By Lee Harris
Published by Fawcett Books:

THE GOOD FRIDAY MURDER
THE YOM KIPPUR MURDER
THE CHRISTENING DAY MURDER
THE ST. PATRICK'S DAY MURDER
THE CHRISTMAS NIGHT MURDER
THE THANKSGIVING DAY MURDER
THE PASSOVER MURDER
THE VALENTINE'S DAY MURDER
THE NEW YEAR'S EVE MURDER
THE LABOR DAY MURDER

THE
LABOR DAY
MURDER

Lee Harris

FAWCETT GOLD MEDAL • NEW YORK

A Fawcett Gold Medal Book
Published by The Ballantine Publishing Group
Copyright © 1998 by Lee Harris

All rights reserved under International and Pan-American Copyright Conventions. Published in the United States by The Ballantine Publishing Group, a division of Random House, Inc., New York, and simultaneously in Canada by Random House of Canada Limited, Toronto.

http://www.randomhouse.com

Library of Congress Catalog Card Number: 98-96035

ISBN 0-449-15017-8

Manufactured in the United States of America

First Edition: August 1998

10 9 8 7 6 5 4 3 2 1

For the other three-quarters
of Nuns, Mothers and Others,
Valerie Wolzien, Lora Roberts, and Jonnie Jacobs,
the best friends, the best companions, the best boosters
a writer could ask for.

The author wishes to thank Ana M. Soler and James L. V. Wegman for their usual excellent information, advice, and criticism, and also Martin and Anita Rich, without whose knowledge of Fire Island and kind invitation to see it firsthand I could not have written this book.

There is no fire without some smoke.
Proverbes
JOHN HEYWOOD
1497–1580

THE
LABOR DAY
MURDER

PROLOGUE

There are words that sear our innards when we hear them, especially if accompanied by a piercing scream. I have heard such words and I remember each instance with the horror they evoked that first moment. The frantic cry of "Mommy!" by a lost or hurt child. "Look out!" shouted as someone steps off a curb. A cry of "Help!" from someone walking a city street on a dark night.

Most recently it was a bloodcurdling scream followed by the single word "Fire!" on a beautiful beach near dusk as summer came to a happy and noisy end. I remember looking toward the town that bordered the beach, then up to where dark smoke was furling like a tornado in the darkening sky and I remember, too, thinking, Those poor people. Their house will never be the same.

I had no idea who the people were or where exactly the house was, except that it was north of where we were standing, and slightly to the west. And I could not have imagined, as the men in the fire brigade started running from the beach, that the house that was burning was the least of it, that much worse had happened than a house fire, that the lives of a small group of people on that island would never be the same after the smoke settled and the water ran off and the truth was uncovered. If it could be uncovered.

* * *

1

And later, when it was dark, there would be the shadow up on the dune, the dusky figure of someone sitting, facing the ocean, and a glow that brightened and waned, brightened and waned. At the beginning, I had no idea who or what it was. At the end, it was what I remembered best.

1

I have always been a child of summer. While others prefer to ski and ice skate, my pleasure is to swim and garden. The house I inherited from Aunt Meg is a stone's throw from the Long Island Sound and since moving in, I've spent many wonderful hours on the little cove nearby, both in and out of the water. But even though we have a big backyard and a wonderful beach, we jumped at the invitation that dropped in our laps one fine spring day.

"Chris," my friend and neighbor Melanie Gross said over the telephone that morning, "something's come up and Hal and I can't use my uncle's house on Fire Island the end of August. Do you think you and Jack and little Eddie would like to go in our place?"

The first thing out of my mouth was, "Fire Island—that's somewhere off Long Island, isn't it?"

"It's a barrier island a few miles off the southern shore of Long Island, a long, skinny strip of land with one village after another, a small state park at the western end, and a lot of park at the eastern end. There are no cars, Jack can leave his jackets and ties at home, it's just a lot of fun and sun and leisure."

"It sounds wonderful. Why aren't you and Hal going?"

"One of his old buddies from law school is getting

3

married in California and we decided to make a vacation out of it. We're flying out a week or so before the wedding, which is Labor Day weekend. And my uncle's going to Europe so he offered us the house. I already asked him if you guys could take it instead."

"It sounds like a dream, Mel. Jack has that last week of August and first week of September off—he put in for it a long time ago—so I know we're free."

"Great. I'll tell Uncle Max it's a deal."

I remember saying, "I should ask Jack first," but Mel pooh-poohed that.

"He'll say yes. I know him."

And she was right. He loved the idea. He said he hadn't been to Fire Island since his wild youth—since he's only a little past thirty I wasn't sure how long ago he was talking about and decided not to ask—and he thought it would be a great place to spend a vacation, especially now that we had Eddie, who would be about nine months old when we went.

For me it was more than a vacation; it was an opportunity to expand my world. Having spent fifteen years of my life in a convent, from the age of fifteen to the age of thirty, I had traveled very little and vacationed mostly with my aunt in the house Jack and I now owned. And although I've been a secular person for three years and married for two of them, I've never quite gotten over all the years of leaving home with fifty cents in my pocket, which meant that a vacation that cost little was very appealing.

So that was how we ended up on Fire Island at the end of August. It was everything Mel had promised, and a lot more. The vacation began on a hot, breezy day in August with the ferry trip from Bay Shore, Long Island out to the island. For about thirty wonderful minutes we crossed the bay out to Blue Harbor, a small community toward the western end of the thirty-two-mile strip of land that was Fire Island. We sat upstairs on the deck for a few minutes and then I took Eddie downstairs and inside, my worries about the bright sun overcoming my strong desire to feel both it and the breeze on my skin.

From the open window we could see the weathered dock and the little gray frame building with the words "Blue Harbor" painted on it. Off to the right, in a kind of breezeway, hung wagon after wagon, the transportation of choice on Fire Island, waiting for their owners to unlock them and load them with luggage. The slightly bumpy end to our voyage as the ferry hit the dock caused a few tears, but Eddie recovered quickly when we put him in his stroller and walked off the boat.

Mel had passed along a ring of necessary keys a few weeks earlier, along with several pages of instructions. We found the family wagon hanging among all the other family carts and wagons and unlocked the padlock with ease. Traveling with a baby meant carrying all sorts of necessities that didn't quite fit in the wagon, but being resourceful people, we distributed things around the stroller and Jack managed to push a suitcase with one hand and pull the wagon with the other as we walked on the narrow lanes and streets to the Margulies house.

The sidewalks, if you could call them that, were all of four feet wide, and with the exception of one or two streets, were made of wood like a boardwalk. The first thing I noticed as we started our walk was that no one seemed to have stairs in this village. Every house we passed had a ramp up to a deck, and people on bicycles, ringing their handlebar bells to signal their approach, zipped up and down the ramps. It was no wonder there were no cars. I've never seen one narrow enough to fit on those streets.

The second thing that drew my attention was the many beautiful, gnarled pine trees that seemed to grow on every lawn, half hiding the houses behind them. And there were tall grasses, maybe as much as ten feet tall or more, that marked property boundaries. Although the houses were not far apart, I could see that looking into your neighbor's yard would not be easy. In other words, there was lots of privacy.

In walking to our vacation home we actually crossed the width of the island from the bay beach on the north to the sea beach on the south in a matter of minutes. About halfway there, we crossed Main Street, the widest street in the village at no more than six or eight feet. This, Mel had told me, was where the Labor Day Parade would go by, something we should not miss. I took a deep breath of the salt breeze and vowed not to miss it.

"Our" house, the one owned by Max Margulies, Mel's paternal uncle, was a grander affair than I had expected. The last house on Park Street, made of wood that had weathered naturally, and mounted on stilts like most of the houses in the village, it sat high on the dune that led to the beach, giving a clear view of the beach and the ocean beyond it. It had two stories, with a wraparound deck on the first floor, and a kind of tower at the right-hand end as you faced it from the dune, a widow's walk circling the tower on the second story. There was a door that I later learned led to the kitchen, and facing the ocean, a front door.

We pulled all our rolling vehicles up the ramp at the back and around to the front door. Inside, we were enchanted. The huge living room that overlooked the deck, the beach, and the Atlantic was furnished in comfortable, cotton-covered chairs and sofas of cane, and the floor, a gleaming affair of polished wood strips, was partly covered with sisal and cotton area rugs. Eddie could crawl to his heart's content without destroying anybody's fine furniture or carpets.

Upstairs there was actually a room with a crib, just as Mel had promised, and there were other bedrooms, including the one with the widow's walk, which would accommodate Jack and me more than comfortably. We dropped our suitcases and went back downstairs to see the rest of the first floor.

The kitchen was a dream. It was the other half of the first floor after the living room, with a large butcher-block table at one end and everything you always wanted in a kitchen at the other end. A Peg-Board near the door to the deck had several hooks on it and I hung our spare house key on one of them. In case we went in different directions, we would each have a key.

"I thought Mel said people lived simply out here," Jack said, as awed as I by the appliances and space.

"I guess Uncle Max thinks this is simplicity. I hope you're still looking forward to cooking."

"Hey, I wouldn't miss it."

We had carried along a plentiful supply of steaks, hamburgers, fish, and other easy-to-grill foods so we wouldn't have to shop locally and pay high prices. On the bay side of the village, Mel had promised, there was a grocery store where we could replenish our resources if we had to, albeit for a price. But this was a great improvement over the situation twenty or more years ago, she had said, when all food had to be imported from the mainland.

We took everything out of the bags and cold box we

had brought and filled the freezer and refrigerator while Eddie explored the kitchen floor and banged a pot noisily.

"I think I'm going to love it," Jack said, as the last item went inside.

I scooped Eddie off the floor and gave him a hug. "I already do," I said.

2

It was a relaxing week with perfect weather and warm sea water. We decided to walk every inch of Blue Harbor and we did, saying hello to everyone we met along the way, a remarkably friendly group of people, mostly homeowners but many just there for the week or weekend.

Next door to us, going back toward the bay, were families that had been coming to Fire Island for years. Across the street were a couple of larger, older houses that the owners had rented out to groups, to the consternation of the nearby owners, and I have to admit, to our own. The people were young and friendly, but they were up late and very noisy. Their garbage overflowed the cans and lay on the ground till it was picked up. There were disagreements between members of the groups that flared into shouting matches, sometimes causing us to burst into laughter. They seemed to argue about the silliest, most mundane things, mostly whose turn it was to do some chore that apparently no one wanted to do.

But when we ran into them on the beach or on the street or in the grocery store over on the bay side, they were smiling and pleasant.

We found the village had a large freshwater pool and I started swimming there every afternoon. Eddie also preferred the freshwater to the salt, and by the end of the week I was sure he was on his way to being a swimmer. Not bad for a little boy who hadn't yet stood on his own two feet!

Jack indulged one of his deepest desires and did all the cooking, a double pleasure for me because I'm not very good at it and I consider it work. I decided not to think about pounds added till we were home, and from the way Jack ate, he must have made the same decision.

On the Saturday that marked a week since our arrival, we started out on a morning walk as we had done each day, waving to our neighbors, the Jorgensens, and then their neighbors, the Wagners. When we reached the bay we took a turn and found ourselves in front of what looked like a firehouse.

"I never thought about community services," I said. "But I guess you can't live without a fire department, even on an island."

"They probably get a kitchen fire every once in a while. Let's go in and show Eddie the fire engine."

The door was open and we went inside. Sure enough, there were two fire trucks in there, bright red with ladders and other equipment, and a couple of smaller vehicles, just like at home in Oakwood. These looked as though they had been polished moments before.

"Good morning," a man's voice said.

I turned to see a nice-looking man in cutoffs and a bright pink shirt walking into the garage with a bucket in one hand and a bunch of rags in the other. "I'm Chris Brooks, and this is my husband, Jack."

The men shook hands.

"I'm Ken Buckley, glad to meet you. And who's this little fella?"

"This is Eddie," Jack said, and Ken Buckley gave our son a practiced tickle that caused giggles.

"I remember when mine were that size," he said with a grin. "A lot less trouble than they are now. You folks renters?"

"We're staying in Max Margulies's house," I said.

"Oh, right. I heard Max was having guests for the end of August. I hope you're staying for Labor Day."

"We are," Jack said. "It's our first vacation in a while and it's been great."

"Nothing's better than Fire Island, and Blue Harbor's as good a village as they come. Don't miss our parade on Monday. It's the last blowout of the season."

"We heard," I said.

"And the party on the beach afterward. Courtesy of the Blue Harbor Fire Department." He held his hands out expansively.

"Of which you're a member."

"Of which I'm chief. Max is one of our inactive members. Basically it means he's over sixty. You turn sixty and you're inactive. Unless we need you." He smiled.

"Where'd you get your training?" Jack asked.

"A fire school on Long Island, very high-tech. We keep pretty up-to-date with drills on the beach. Haven't had a fire since two summers ago when some weekend renters smoked in bed."

"Were they all right?" I asked.

"We got them out but the house was a mess. Everything's wood around here and it had been a dry month. What wasn't burned was soaked. Anyway, that's history. How're you enjoying Max's mansion?"

I left Jack to banter while I showed Eddie the fire engines. These were the first motorized vehicles I'd seen since we got off the ferry. Even the taxis around here were boats, and I wondered how something as big as these fire engines could get around.

When Eddie lost interest, I went back to where the two men were still chatting. "I hope we didn't leave any prints on your nice, clean fire engines," I said.

"Not to worry. They'll be gleaming for the parade."

"How do you move them around the village? The streets must be too narrow and most of them are made of wood."

"We've got a concrete street that crosses from the bay to the ocean and Main Street runs from east to west. Otherwise, we use the beach. If we get stuck in the sand—and we do—forty of us get together and lift 'er right up."

Jack and I laughed. "That must be something to see."

"Won't happen at the parade. We'll roll right down Main Street."

"We'll be there," Jack said.

"How big a parade could it be?" I asked, when we were back outside. "It's such a small community."

"Roughly three hundred fifty houses," Jack said. "He was telling me about it while you were leaving prints on his fire engines. About fourteen hundred people, less during the week, more on the weekends. But it's close to capacity right now. Even the men take the end of August off."

"Even cops."

"Cops who thought ahead and put in for the time when the snow was this high." He held his hand at a level I had never seen snow reach. "He said Mel's Uncle Max was the chief back in the Eighties for a few years. He made it sound like the firemen are some kind of royalty. Anyway, there'll be a high school band from the mainland and then late in the afternoon, the party."

"Do we need tickets?"

"He said it's the fire company's gift to the community."

"Sounds great. Let's walk over to the store and get

some milk before they're all sold out. It's a big weekend and everyone's going to want to cook."

"Especially me."

Happily, I had married the right man.

On Sunday the Jorgensens invited us over to share their barbecue dinner. I got Eddie ready for bed and stretched out the stroller in their house, and he cooperated by falling asleep. We stayed late, listening to tales of towns growing, gossip about people we didn't know, and descriptions of past parades and post-parade parties.

"Those firemen have it good," Marti Jorgensen said, as we sat in the light of anti-bug torches after dinner. "But they give back, which is nice."

"What do you mean, they 'have it good'?" I asked.

"It's a social thing, you know, being a fireman. They get together every week and have a good time. The department is insured by a company that pays back Fire Island two percent of the premiums for what's called 'benevolent purposes for local fire departments.' In plain English that means beer money." Everyone laughed and Marti went on. "It's about three thousand dollars a year, so it's a lot of beer. I guess they use some of it for the party though. That costs more than five thousand."

"That's an expensive party," I said, always the penny-pincher.

"It's fun," her husband, Al, said. "It's the end of the season, everyone's feeling good. After Labor Day things calm down, the ferries don't run as often, the groups go home, and by fall there's only about twenty families left, mostly couples. We've been out here in the winter a few times and it's eerie."

"Are the other towns like this one? We've walked into two of them but haven't looked around much."

"Every town has its own character," Al said. He took a sip of the cognac he had poured for himself and Jack. "Green Bay's the richest one, lot of celebrities living there. Silver Beach is gay."

"A whole town is gay?" I said with surprise.

"Well, I can't vouch for every person there, but that's the reputation. It's a very old community. They've been coming to the island, I'd guess, since before the Second World War. Nobody bothers them."

I found it very interesting. I leaned back in my chair and listened as Al spoke. This town, that fire department, the senator's son, the deer encroaching from the park at the end of the island, the need to repost the house, the winds, the tide. Still I felt myself drifting off.

"Al, that's just gossip," I heard Marti say firmly. "You shouldn't talk about it."

"It's not gossip if it's true. And it's true. We all know it."

I was alert but had no idea what they were talking about.

"I think my wife's falling asleep," Jack said. "And missing the juiciest stuff."

"What did I miss?"

"Who's-sleeping-with-whom gossip," my husband said.

"The fire chief has a well-earned reputation," Al said, taking another sip of his cognac.

"We just met him yesterday at the firehouse. Nice-looking man."

"That's what the ladies say."

"It's really a small town, isn't it?"

"Very small," Marti said. "And the houses are close together. Al always says when you tell a joke in one house, the people next door laugh. But it can work against you." She looked rather grim.

"He seemed like a friendly man," I said.

"Too friendly." Al didn't want to let it go.

"He's done wonders as fire chief," Marti said, as though to move on to a more favorable side of Ken Buckley. "They've come to every house to inspect the kitchens, they've given us all good tips on grilling out of doors. And of course, they throw the best party of the year." She smiled.

"Well, we'll be there." Jack stood up and stretched. "I think we should pick up our son and make our long way home." "Home" was about twenty feet away.

I was glad he'd made the first move. Ten minutes later, Eddie was in his crib and we were getting ready for bed.

The next morning Eddie ate his cereal with gusto and drank his milk from the silver cup St. Stephen's Convent had given him at his baptism. His little teeth were making fine scratches and dents in the rim, which my mother's old friend Elsie Rivers assured me made it a keepsake. When he was happily crawling on the floor, Jack and I sat down to our breakfast. It was Labor Day and the parade was at ten, giving us lots of time to eat, dress, and walk over to Main Street.

"Sorry I missed the revelations last night," I said. "I must have drifted off."

"You did. Al obviously has a grudge against Ken Buckley."

"Maybe Buckley invaded a friend's territory."

"Could be. The way Al describes him, he's a real ladies' man."

"He was so sweet to Eddie, I thought of him as fatherly."

"The two aren't mutually exclusive. Buckley said he had kids. But it sounds as though his philandering is well documented."

"I can't see how you could carry on an affair in a town as tiny as this one."

"There's the big city everyone goes home to eventually. Don't forget that."

"Well, I'll give him the benefit of the doubt. He made my son giggle."

Jack gave me a grin and went back to his breakfast.

We got to Main Street in plenty of time. People of all ages were already lining up in front of the houses that faced the street. It had rained last night and there were still small pools of water under the houses. You didn't need to know much else to understand why so many were on stilts and basements were nonexistent.

I heard the band from a distance and turned to look. They looked pretty spiffy, with a high-stepping baton twirler at the front and plenty of brass following him. Al had told us that the band played for the privilege of spending the day on the Blue Harbor beach and attending the party. There were a good-looking bunch of teenagers from a school called Bishop Palermo.

"Look at the band, Eddie," I said, holding him up to see.

The band was followed by the fire engines and other vehicles, which just barely made it down Main Street. Several young firemen were aboard, waving and tossing candy to the children in the crowd.

Behind the trucks came the rest of the firemen, led by Chief Buckley, all in spanking new uniforms. As they marched by, I became aware that off to my left there was a smattering of applause that seemed to be moving along toward me as the parade advanced. I stood on my toes, trying to see what was coming, but couldn't see anything.

"What are they clapping for?" I asked a teenaged girl standing near me.

"Probably Chief La Coste. They always give him a good round."

"Is he a local hero?"

"He's everybody's hero," she said. "He's the oldest man on Fire Island. He's ninety-two."

"Wow."

"Yeah. He lives out here all year long. He was fire chief back around World War Two. Or One. I'm not sure."

At that age, it could conceivably have been either. I handed Eddie off to Jack and looked for the old chief. I knew he couldn't be far because the applause was rippling its way toward me. Finally, as the girl beside me started clapping, I saw him.

He was a weathered old man, thin, walking as upright as the men half his age. He was wearing an ancient uniform with silver braid on the sleeves, and with great aplomb, he smiled and waved to his fans. I clapped along with everyone else and leaned over to tell Jack who he was. I thought it was pretty amazing that someone his age would be marching instead of sitting comfortably in a fire engine.

The parade was concluded with a children's parade, the little ones dressing up in costumes almost as if it were Halloween. They were quite inventive and we gave them a lot of applause as they passed. As the last of the parade went by, everyone standing on Main Street fell in behind the marchers and we all ended up at the firehouse where there was punch and cookies, presumably to tide us over till the real party.

Eddie thought the sugar cookies were pretty terrific and I took an extra one for later. We hung around, talking to people who lived in Blue Harbor and to the band members who couldn't wait to put their bathing suits on and jump in the water. I couldn't blame them. It was a warm day and I was looking forward to cooling off myself.

After a while, we walked home and I fed Eddie and put him down for his afternoon nap. The party was scheduled for late afternoon, which would give him a chance to sleep and me a chance for a swim. A good way to spend Labor Day.

3

It was a great party. The food stretched for what seemed like miles under a huge tent set on the beach. I could understand why it was such an expensive affair when I saw the amount of food and tasted it. It was truly a feast. Then there was the open bar under a separate tent, with a steady stream of people, mostly men, filling and refilling their glasses.

The party was about two blocks down the beach from us, so the noise was less noticeable in our house. When we decided we'd had enough, we'd be able to sleep. I had the feeling this was going to be an all-night affair for some, or at least until the food and alcohol ran out.

The Jorgensens were there, and members of the fire department, most of them now in casual, hot-weather clothes. Ken Buckley remembered me and stopped to talk for a minute. When he left, I sought out the old man, Chief La Coste, and introduced myself to him.

"Hope you're enjoying your vacation," he said. "That's a nice house you're staying in. Max built it himself about twenty years ago."

"It's wonderful. Where do you live?"

"Over on North Avenue. My house is a little smaller than yours. And a lot older. But it suits me."

"I heard you live here all year round."

"This is the only home I've got. I like it even better in

19

the winter. Not so many strangers around." He gave me a quick smile. "I didn't mean you, ma'am. It's all these young folks that rent a house and come out for the weekends. They're not as careful as they could be with the property, if you understand what I mean."

I did and I said something sympathetic. It was the old tug of war between the generations. They got on each others' nerves.

"Hard to be tolerant when they don't respect the rights of others. Bunch of damned noisemakers, if you ask me."

"But they'll be gone soon," I said, to soothe him.

"Not soon enough. How long are you staying?"

"Till the end of the week. My husband's a police officer in New York and he's studying law at night. His school starts next week."

"Well, you come round tomorrow and we'll have a little talk," he said with a smile. "Things'll be calmed down by then. Just ask anyone where Chief La Coste's house is. They all know."

"Thank you. I look forward to it."

Jack and I stuffed ourselves with food, enjoying it and having a good time. Eddie's dinner and bath schedule would go by the board today but he seemed to be enjoying himself as much as we were, what with people stopping to talk to him.

Suddenly there was a long, high-pitched scream and the voices around us stopped. "Fire!" the screamer shouted. "There's a fire! Look! Look at the smoke!"

We all looked toward the houses of the town and there, off to the left, was an ugly funnel of dark smoke. The firemen didn't wait to be told; they ran. As they headed toward the firehouse, a wailing siren sounded.

"I don't like the look of this," Chief La Coste said at my side.

"Looks like big trouble," I agreed. "Can the Blue Harbor company handle it?"

"The companies from the neighboring villages will join them. Hear that? That's another siren. They'll be here. They'll get it under control."

"I hope so." I spotted Jack, who was carrying Eddie. Eddie was crying. Sirens scared him, but there was nowhere to go to avoid them.

"I'll look for you tomorrow," the old man said, reminding me that we had an invitation.

"Thank you, I'll be there." Then I ran across the sand to Jack.

Along with most of the town, we headed for the fire. By the time we got there, the Blue Harbor firemen and two other companies were already pouring water from hoses attached to hydrants onto the burning house.

"It's the chief's house," I heard someone say excitedly behind me, and I looked around for the old man I had been talking to on the beach, but couldn't find him.

"Chief La Coste?" I asked the man.

"No, Ken Buckley. I hope his family's outta there."

I hoped so, too. I looked for him, but all the firemen were now in their heavy jackets and hats and I couldn't recognize anyone. "Someone says it's Chief Buckley's house," I told Jack.

"They look like they know what they're doing. There's probably no one inside. Everyone's at the beach. Or they were."

"Everyone" seemed to be at the scene right now. I wondered if the chief's children were on the island, whether they might have stayed behind in the house while their parents were at the party. The thought gave me an unpleasant sensation in the pit of my stomach.

"Let's get Eddie out of here," Jack said. "I don't want him breathing the smoke."

"I'll walk back to the tent. He doesn't seem very tired. You can stay here if you want. If I'm not on the beach, I'll be back at the house."

"I'll hang around here for a while." He looked concerned. He leaned over and kissed both of us.

"Come on, Eddie," I said. "Let's go back and watch the sun set."

I eased my way through the crowd, watching the firemen as I went. Each town wore slightly different uniforms, I noticed, and they worked together as though they had trained that way. I hoped they would get inside to see if any of the Buckley children were there.

As I was strolling my way through the crowd, I felt a hand push me aside. It was a girl with what looked like a fireman's yellow-striped coat pulled over her head. As she turned her head my way, I recognized her.

"Tina," I said. She was a member of the group renting the house closest to ours. "Are you all right?"

She looked at me almost with horror, her diamond stud earrings picking up the last light of the day, and then dashed away, pushing herself through the crowd with her head down. Instinctively, I followed in her wake, clutching Eddie to my shoulder. She moved very quickly out of and then beyond the crowd, finally darting between two houses in a direction I realized would take her more directly to the house she was sharing.

Something made me go after her. She never looked back and it certainly looked as though she were running away from something. All of a sudden she came up against a chain-link fence, and she uttered the loudest "Shit!" I had ever heard in my life. She repeated it several times, pounding the fence and sounding more hysterical with each rendition.

"Tina, can I help?" I called, standing away out of fear that she might turn her anger on me, and not anxious to walk through grass that might hold ticks.

She looked back then, and I could see that her face was smudged with dirt, her eyes wide. "No!" she screamed, and took off around the other side of the house.

I gave up and walked back to her group's house, using the more conventional streets. The front door was open, which was not unusual, but no one was around. I stood quietly and listened. The whole area seemed deserted. If Tina had come home, she was keeping still.

I turned toward the beach and walked back to where the happy party had been in full swing less than half an hour before.

The tent was not entirely deserted. A woman had taken the place of the fireman bartender and was filling glasses. Several women were behind the tables of food, whether to help serve or to guard the food I wasn't sure.

"Is it really Ken Buckley's house?" one of them called to me.

"That's what I was told."

"Anyone inside?" Her face looked tense.

"I don't know. I was only there a few minutes."

"There's a lot of smoke, isn't there." It wasn't a question. "Why don't you help yourself to some dinner? Before the crowds come back. I'll hold the baby if you like." She smiled, but Eddie would have none of it.

"He's getting tired," I said. "I'll fill a plate and take it home. Thanks for the offer."

By the time Jack got back, I was back down in the living room with my book.

"You guys OK?"

"We're fine. Is the fire out?"

"Looks like it. They'll stick around for a while to make sure. Someone died in the fire, Chris."

"Oh, no. A child?"

"The chief. They brought Ken Buckley's body out a little while ago."

"How terrible." I felt my eyes fill. "Did he die fighting the fire?"

"He wasn't in uniform. Looked like he was sleeping. They found him on his bed."

"I saw him at the party, Jack."

"You sure?"

"Absolutely. We said hello."

"Maybe he was tired. Maybe he didn't feel so good. He must've gone home and gone to bed."

"I wonder."

"About what?"

"You know that grouper house just down the street? The one across from the Wagners?"

"Yeah. We've said hello a couple of times."

"I saw Tina from that house. She was at the fire and she was trying to get away from it as fast and inconspicuously as possible." I described how she had been dressed, with the heavy fireman's coat pulled over her head, how her face, when I finally saw it at the fence, had been smudged with smoky grime.

"You trying to make this sound ominous or am I just reading big trouble into this?"

"I'm just telling you what I saw. I lost her at the fence. I was carrying Eddie and didn't want to run a race to follow her. When I got to the house, either no one was there or they were being very quiet."

"For a change."

"Yes."

"You think she could have been inside the house during the fire?"

"How else did she get so dirty and sooty-looking?"

He looked at his watch. "If this was arson—"

It hadn't occurred to me. "Would an arsonist stay around while the fire's burning?"

"He might, but it's too late to stop the ferry if he took off. There was one that left right after we saw the smoke. It's already landed. So much for keeping everyone on the island."

"You really think it's arson?"

"You'd expect a fire chief to obey the safety rules better than anyone else."

"Maybe he was smoking in bed."

"I think I'll find the local cop tomorrow morning and talk to him. Just to make him aware."

"You know what I think I'll do? I'll walk over to the group house and talk to Tina. If she hasn't gotten on a ferry back to the mainland."

"Good idea. I'll baby-sit."

There were lights on all over the house when I got there. I went up the ramp and knocked on the open door. No one heard me. I leaned inside and called, "Hello."

A girl in bare feet, shorts, and a big T-shirt came out of the back of the house. "Hi."

"Hi. I'm Chris."

"From the big house on the dune."

"Right. Is Tina here?"

"I think she's upstairs."

"Can I talk to her?"

She went to the stairs and called, "Tina? You up there?"

A young man in bathing trunks walked by and gave me a smile.

The girl who had called upstairs came back. "She's there. It's the room at the front of the house."

I went upstairs and knocked on the door.

"Yeah?"

I opened the door and went in. Tina was sitting on an old easy chair painting her nails a shade of brown. "I'm Chris from the house across the street."

"Yeah. Hi."

"I wanted to ask you about the fire."

"What about it?"

"Were you in the house when the fire started?"

She looked confused. "No. Why?"

"When I saw you, it looked as though you were coming out of the house."

"You saw me? Where?"

"In front of Chief Buckley's house."

"You must have me confused with someone else." She dipped her brush in the small bottle, wiped it carefully on the side, and started another nail, keeping her eyes on her task.

"I saw you, Tina. You were walking away from the burning house. You had a fireman's coat over you. I asked you if you were all right."

"Sorry," she said, looking up from her work. "I just don't remember. I was walking on the beach this afternoon. I saw the smoke but I didn't go to the fire. I hate crowds."

I turned around and left the room.

"She's a good liar," I said to Jack, after I told him what had happened.

"So you're sure it was Tina you saw."

"Right down to her diamond earrings. I called her by name when she looked at me. She's cleaned herself up and changed her clothes and made up a story. It doesn't mean she's an arsonist but I bet she knows something about that fire."

"You know her last name?"

"If I heard it, I don't remember it."

"We'll get it in the morning. Let's turn in."

4

We were having our breakfast the next morning when there was a knock on the kitchen door. Jack got up to open it and Marti Jorgensen came in.

"Have you heard the news?" she asked.

"You mean about the fire?" I said. "Jack told me Chief Buckley died."

"He was murdered."

"Wow," I said, feeling a shiver. "Join us for a cup of coffee." I pulled out a chair and got another mug.

"Then it was arson," Jack said.

"I don't know about arson. He has a bullet in him. That's murder." She leaned over and called to Eddie. "What's a nice little boy doing on the floor? Come and sit on Marti's lap."

Eddie gave her a big smile and allowed himself to be lifted.

"There we go. What a sweetheart you are." She turned to me. "If you feel like dropping him off, Chris, I wouldn't mind looking after him for a couple of hours. He's just the age I like."

"Thank you. Maybe I'll take advantage of your offer. Marti, when we were over the other night, Al was telling tales about Chief Buckley and you seemed very uncomfortable about what he was saying."

"It's just that I hate to gossip." She smoothed Eddie's curls with loving fingers. "Al carried a grudge against Ken, a personal thing. I don't want to go into it. I'm sure he was right in what he was saying. Ken was known to be a ladies' man. To be honest, it was more than that. I don't know why Eve stayed with him. I don't know how their winters were—we only saw each other in the summer—but he earned his reputation. He had girlfriends. I even know who some of them were."

"So, lots of suspects." Jack said.

"Don't be silly," Marti said with a smile. "It probably wasn't any more important to the women than it was to Ken. Something to do in the summer, that's all. Certainly nothing to kill over."

"Is his wife on the island?" I asked.

"I don't really know but I would guess so. She's always involved in the Labor Day Party."

"Do you happen to know who this summer's girlfriend was?"

She looked embarrassed. "I don't. I don't even know if there was one. You could talk to Al."

"Marti, do you know the group in the house across the street from you?"

"I wish I didn't. I could kill the Kleins for renting out their house to those people. This used to be such a nice family town. I hate seeing all the big old houses given over to people who don't take care of them. Not to mention the noise."

"Do you know any of the people in that house?"

"We say 'hello' and I ask them politely to keep their garbage in the cans. That's about it. I think ten of them rented the house together."

"Are they all couples?"

"I wouldn't know. Sometimes they're couples at the

beginning of the summer and not at the end. Or they're different couples by Labor Day. Why do you ask?"

"I thought I saw one of them at the fire."

"Al said everyone in Blue Harbor was at the fire. Except me. I get too upset."

Eddie was playing with Marti's beads but she didn't seem to mind. She whispered to him and he giggled.

"Would you mind if I talked to Al?"

"Not at all. He'd probably love the chance to tell what he knows. Are you planning to write about this?"

"No. I'm just interested."

"Talk to Chief La Coste. He knows everything that's happened in Blue Harbor for the last sixty years."

"He invited us over for today. Did I tell you that, Jack? Maybe that's a good place to start."

"And leave this honey with me. You'll be doing me a favor."

I promised Marti I would take up her baby-sitting offer in the next day or so. Jack decided to visit the police station while I looked in on the chief. When Eddie got tired later in the morning, I put him in the stroller and by the time we were halfway down the block, he had fallen asleep. I had looked up Chief La Coste in the little phone book, as small a phone book as I had ever seen, and found the number of his house. North Avenue was one block from the bay, the bay being on the north side of the island. We turned east and walked a couple of blocks till we found it. Almost hidden behind thick pines and willows, it was an old house, weathered gray, with black shutters that appeared to be real. They could be shut to cover the windows but they were all fastened in an open position today. I went up the ramp and knocked on the front door.

"Well, glad to see you, Chris. Come right in." The chief was expansive, helping me over the threshold with the stroller. "Little feller seems to be sleeping. We can go sit out back, and he can get his fresh air and we'll have a glass of lemonade."

"Can I help you with anything, Chief?"

"No, no. Just make yourself comfortable. People tell me I'm old so they come and do nice things for me they wouldn't't've thought to do when I was young and lazy. Like making sure I've got lemonade. Comes fresh every morning."

We went through the small house and out the back door and sat on the weathered deck. I poured the lemonade into brightly painted plastic glasses and passed one to the chief. Eddie slept in a shady corner while we talked.

"I guess you heard about the tragedy," the chief said, holding his glass between his palms to cool them. The day was already warm and muggy, except for the breeze.

"We went over to Chief Buckley's house when we saw the smoke."

"You and everybody else. That was some crowd. They did a good job, the three fire departments. Saved a lot of the house. Too bad Ken died. A man half my age dies, I feel for him."

"Did you know it was murder?" I asked.

"Heard this morning. Can't imagine who would want to kill Ken Buckley."

"Maybe he made someone angry," I suggested. I wasn't sure whether to talk about what we had learned from Marti. If Chief La Coste didn't know about the philandering, I wasn't going to be the one to tell him.

The chief laughed. "He made a lot of people angry.

Don't mean they're gonna kill him. Nowadays everybody thinks of guns first. You can settle your grievances by talking. Talking'll take you a long way."

"It probably wasn't a robbery," I said.

"Nah. We don't have much of that here. We all leave our doors open. Of course, with the groups that come out now, you never can tell."

"No one seems to have a good word for the groups."

"Except those that rent their houses to them. Get a lotta income from that. Course, you have to clean up after them and make repairs. It's not all profit."

"You must know all the homeowners, Chief. You've been out here a long time."

"Over sixty years. Me and my wife built this house with our own four hands. Almost lost it in the hurricane of 'thirty-eight. That was somethin', I can tell you. Every other house you could see was lost. In the summer of 'thirty-nine they had to rebuild the whole town."

"Except this house."

"Right. Except this house." He took a drink of his lemonade and stared off. "And I remember the other disaster, the biggest fire they ever had on Fire Island, right here in Blue Harbor, 'bout fifteen, sixteen years ago. Nothing left of that house except the chimney."

"Was anyone hurt?"

"They were lucky. Lost everything except their lives. Nothin' left to pack up. They got on the ferry and never came back."

"And the chimney?"

"Stood there a coupla years till someone bought the property and put up a new house."

"You have quite a memory," I said.

"Yup. My brain's in better shape than any other organ in my body. I remember everything. I remember folks that came and went; folks that stayed for thirty, forty years; little babies that grew up here and then built themselves houses for their own families. And I know where all the bodies are buried." He smiled and it struck me that his teeth might be his own. They were uneven, off-color, with gaps between them, hardly what you'd pay for from a professional.

"I suppose it's easy to bring a gun onto the island."

"No metal detectors that I know of at the ferry dock. Bring anything on board you can carry."

"When did the Buckleys first come to Blue Harbor?"

"Let's see. If I remember right, they rented a house the first couple of summers, kind of a dumpy old house on the other side of town. Then the Mayfields' house went on the market and they bought it right away."

"Is that the house that just burned?"

"That's the one. Nice house. Three bedrooms upstairs. Mine here's all on one floor. They got a nice kitchen that they fixed up themselves. Nice big deck. Not as big a house as Max's, but a real comfortable house to live in."

I looked over at Eddie, who was sleeping peacefully.

"Nice little boy you've got there," the old man said.

"Thank you. I'm a former nun and sometimes I'm still surprised to find myself a wife and mother."

"Maybe that's why you've got such nice manners," Chief La Coste said. "We raised three of our own."

"How many years have you lived out here all year round?"

"Quite a while now. Must be twenty years anyway. Long as you've got heat and light and a place to buy food, it's a great place to live."

"Do you have any idea who might have killed Ken Buckley?"

"Well, I don't know. For myself, I thought he was a wonderful human being. But it could have been an unhappy wife, an unhappy mistress." He looked over at me. "Oh, yes, I know about his love life. Aren't too many folks on the island who don't."

"Maybe an unhappy husband," I suggested.

"Could be that, too. You see, it could be almost anybody. You helping the police find the killer?"

"I'm just helping myself. I'm curious. I saw Ken Buckley at the party on the beach not long before we saw smoke. That means he went home when the party was just getting going. I wonder if someone was waiting for him there with the gun."

"You know what he was wearing when he was killed?"

"Shorts, I think." I tried to remember what he had looked like on the beach, and all I could see was the pink T-shirt of the firehouse.

The chief laughed. "He was buck naked when they found him."

I thought again of Tina. Had he gone home for a tryst with a girl half his age? "Tell me, Chief, do firemen usually keep their jackets at home?"

"You mean the turnout gear, the big, heavy coats with the yellow safety stripes? Those are kept at the firehouse with the helmets and boots."

"That's what I thought."

"Come on, girl. Let me in on it. You're asking these questions because you saw something."

"I saw someone leaving Chief Buckley's house with a fireman's jacket over her—I mean the turnout coat." I told him the story. He listened very attentively till I had finished.

"I see why you're so interested. Does sound like she

knows a thing or two. What house did you say she was living in?"

"The Kleins'."

"The Kleins'. Over there." He nodded as though fixing the location. "Kleins've owned that house a long time. Their kids got married but they weren't ready to sell yet. So they started renting last year. You know what that does to the population? Instead of two nice, quiet people, you got ten noisy ones. And it's happening all over Blue Harbor."

His interest was obviously in the town, not the murder, but I tried to bring him back. "My husband, Jack, is talking to the police this morning. He thinks they should question her before she leaves Fire Island."

"Sounds like a good idea. You wanna know if she was Ken's girlfriend? Could be. He liked 'em young. So what's your theory? She meets him at his house with a gun, shoots him, and runs away with his turnout coat over her?"

"Maybe."

"And you recognized her, so there goes her alibi of walking on the beach. I'll give you my opinion. I don't think she did it, whoever she is. Ken was nice to his girlfriends."

"But he never left his wife for any of them."

"Never left her. That's the truth."

Eddie was starting to stir. I got up and walked over to the stroller. He whimpered a little.

"I think it's time to go. Let me wash up."

"There's no washing up to do." He gave me a smile. "I've got a nice little girl comes in here in the afternoon, washes my dishes and gets my supper together. Now, is it worth getting old, or what?"

"It's certainly worth it, and you seem to have more fun

at your age than a lot of people do when they're much younger."

"That's just what I say, young lady."

We waited till Eddie had eaten his lunch and gone for his afternoon nap before we sat down for our own lunch and a talk.

"It's not exactly a police department," Jack said, emphasizing the last word. "It's one part-time cop who spends the rest of his life running the restaurant at the bay. Before he came here he was a cop in a small mid-west town."

"That's an interesting combination of careers."

"I was kinda thinking I might like it myself," Jack said with a grin. "The truth is, he's little more than a security guard with the title of chief and a permit to carry a gun, but he doesn't carry it. And he doesn't have a radio car because there aren't any cars. There also doesn't seem to be much crime. He brought in the county people for this."

"Did you tell him about Tina?"

"Right off the bat. The cop called the owners of the house, people named Klein, I think. They had no problem with our searching the house but they're not living there so their permission wouldn't stand up in court. We walked over and talked to the people there, including Tina Frisch. She's pretty young, Chris. I'd guess less than twenty-five."

"I know. Chief La Coste said Ken Buckley liked them young."

"Well, everyone there agreed to let us search their rooms and we did."

"But?"

"Nothing. No fireman's coat for sure. I went over Tina's room myself. It wasn't there."

"And the coat closet?"

"Not much in it. It's summer. No one had brought a coat. There were some umbrellas and a couple of beach chairs, but that was about it."

"She must have gotten rid of it. Did either of you question her?"

"The cop did. His name's Curt Springer, nice guy, seems capable. He sat down with her in the dining room and I sat in the kitchen and listened. He didn't get anything out of her. This trip, she's been here about as long as we have and she's going home at the end of the week. She works in New York in a law office and she's been coming out alternate weekends. That's how they manage to have ten renters. Half the group came out for the Fourth of July, the other half for Labor Day."

"Did she come with a boyfriend?"

"Apparently not. She and two other girls made the arrangement to rent with two other groups. One group is some guys, the other, couples."

"I guess they expected to meet people out here."

"It's been known to happen," my husband said with a twinkle. "What did you get from the old chief?"

"A lot of memories and reminiscences and a glass of freshly made lemonade." I filled him in on all the recollections I could remember, having made some notes as soon as I was home.

"The hurricane of 'thirty-eight," Jack said. "I'm impressed."

"I can't vouch for the accuracy but he sounded authentic. I didn't have the feeling he was rambling. In fact, it was just the opposite. He stated things without much elaboration." As I spoke, I saw Marti walk by the house with a folding chair. It was beach time.

"What do you want to do with this?" Jack asked.

"I don't know. If I hadn't seen Tina leaving that fire, I might be willing to let it alone. She's lying or covering up and it sounds as though she didn't give anything away to the chief cop."

"She came off sounding like a New York girl who got together with friends and friends of friends to have a good time this summer. Pretty ordinary, pretty run-of-the-mill, especially for the young people that come out here."

"So if you believe her, I'm the weird one."

"And that bothers you."

"I think I'll put my bathing suit on and go out on the beach. Marti's out there. Maybe I can talk to her. You mind baby-sitting?"

Jack yawned. "Maybe I'll just get myself a little shut-eye. When Eddie gets up, we'll join you on the beach. If you're still there."

"I'll take the umbrella. Carry a little shade with me."

The beach itself was below the dune on which the house rested. Sparse tall grasses grew on it, and paths down to the beach were marked with the kind of fencing people put up to protect shrubs in winter.

Marti was sitting under her own umbrella, reading a book. She was probably in her fifties, a woman with a good body and gently graying hair. She was alone and as soon as she saw me, she closed her book so I didn't feel intrusive.

"What are you up to?" she said, as I opened my own chair and set up my umbrella in the sand.

"I talked to Chief La Coste this morning. What a memory that man has."

"He's remarkable, that's for sure. Did he know about the murder?"

"He did. I got the feeling there isn't much he doesn't know."

"You're right."

"He told me about the hurricane of 'thirty-eight and the last big fire."

"I almost forgot about that. We were out here that summer. There wasn't anything left of that house except the chimney. Even after they cleaned up the property, that old chimney stood there like a ghost. It gave me the creeps."

"Was Ken Buckley the chief when it happened?"

"Oh, no. He's only been chief a couple of years. I don't remember who it was back then."

"Do you know if Mrs. Buckley is on the island?"

"She is. I heard she was here last night when the house burned."

"Was she in the house?"

"No. She was on the beach at the party when the fire started. I heard from someone this morning that she's staying with her sister and brother-in-law, who also have a house here in Blue Harbor. Mary and Bill Tyler. I don't know how long she'll stay. I suppose she'll go back soon for the funeral. What an awful thing to happen."

We talked for a while and then we both went into the water. The sea was almost warm, the temperature having inched up all summer. I tried to swim but the waves were too much for me. Marti said she enjoyed just jumping into the waves. After a while, we went back to our chairs. When I was dry, I climbed up the dune and went home.

* * *

The little town phone book had an address for William A. Tyler. Since everything was near everything else, I knew it wouldn't be more than a ten-minute walk. Jack agreed to stay home and take Eddie to the pool when he woke up, and I took off. I wasn't looking forward to talking to the new widow, but if the police didn't think there was anything strange about my encounter with Tina, then no one would pursue it.

The Tylers' house looked like the ones on either side except that theirs had a red door that stood open. I liked that. Two adult tricycles were parked on the deck near the front door, probably indicating visitors. I knocked, but no one answered. If they were in the back of the house, they would hardly hear a tap on the door. I opened the screen and stuck my head in. "Hello?" I called.

A woman came running. "Sorry, I didn't hear you. I'm Mary Ellen Tyler."

"I'm Chris Bennett Brooks. My husband and I are spending a couple of weeks in Max Margulies's house."

"Oh, Max, of course. Did you want to see Eve?"

"I've never met her but I want to ask her something. Maybe I can talk to you first and you can tell me whether she's up to a conversation."

"Sure. Come in." She led me into a large room that doubled as living room and dining room and we sat at a big oak table.

I could hear voices from the deck out back. "Mrs. Tyler, I was outside the Buckleys' house yesterday during the fire. I didn't know it was their house till I got there and heard people talking. A few minutes after I arrived, a girl from one of the group houses near the Margulies house pushed her way through the crowd away from the house. She had a fireman's turnout coat over her back and head as though she wanted to hide her face. When she looked at me, I saw that her face was smudged with dirt and grime, as though she'd been inside a smoky house."

Mary Ellen Tyler's forehead was creased into a frown. "Have you told the police chief this?"

"My husband told Chief Springer this morning. My husband is a detective sergeant with NYPD. Tina denies that she was there and she told me to my face that she spent the afternoon walking on the beach, that she never saw me at all. But she did and she was there."

"Let me get my sister." She went out back and the conversation stopped.

A moment later, Eve Buckley joined me at the table. "I'm Eve," she said, extending her hand. She was a woman in her forties, not too tall, with a sweet face and short black hair with a first hint of gray. She looked tired and colorless, perhaps because she wore no makeup, but her eyes were not red and her voice was strong.

"I'm Chris. I'm sorry for your loss."

"Thank you."

"I've been telling your sister what happened yesterday during the fire."

"She told me. Who is this girl?"

"Her name is Tina Frisch." I told her about seeing her during the fire.

"None of this rings a bell. Did you see her coming out of our house?"

"I didn't actually see her coming from the house. I saw her pushing her way through the crowd with her head down. She actually pushed me, which is when I saw her face. I was carrying my baby and we were going home, so I kind of followed her. She was agitated and eventually I lost her. I went to see her last night and she was very calm and denied that we had met outside your house."

"The name doesn't mean anything to me. What does she look like?"

"Slim, light hair, straight and loose. Kind of pale skin. She must not sit in the sun much."

"And she's living in the Kleins' house?"

"Yes. It's just down the street from where we're staying. Did your husband keep his fireman's turnout coat at home?"

"I'm sure he didn't. The turnout gear is always at the firehouse. I certainly didn't see one at home yesterday. Of course, I was in and out, setting up for the party."

"I saw your husband at the party," I said.

"So did I." I thought she sounded rueful. "He didn't tell me he was going home."

"Are you sure—?" I hesitated. "Are you sure it was your husband who died?"

"I'm sure. I identified him." She swallowed hard, as though the identification had been harder than the fact of his death.

"I'm terribly sorry," I said.

"Thank you. I appreciate your coming here. I hadn't heard anything about this girl."

"Chief Springer searched the Kleins' house this morning—my husband participated—looking for the coat. It wasn't there."

"So she got rid of it last night."

"It looks that way. They didn't find any guns either."

"It's certainly very puzzling."

"I'm going to ask the people in town some questions. If I need to get in touch with you, may I call?"

"Of course." She wrote her name and address on a notepad and ripped off the top sheet.

I wrote my two addresses on the next sheet and gave it to her. Then I shook her hand again and left.

Mary Ellen Tyler walked me to the front door. "Were you being discreet or don't you know?" she asked.

I wasn't sure how to answer. "I was discreet but I'm

not sure how much I know. I've been told that Ken was less than faithful."

"That's a kind way to put it. He gave my sister plenty of reasons to get a divorce but she never did it."

"Do you think—or know—that Tina Frisch was a girl-friend of his?"

"I don't know. And I have a feeling from watching Eve as she was talking to you that she doesn't know either. The last woman I saw him with was a rather attractive lawyer in her early thirties. She was out here early in the season but I haven't seen her since the beginning of August. So maybe it ended and she decided not to come back. I haven't talked to Eve about her."

"Was she with a group?"

"No, she rented a small house by herself over on Sunset Parkway. She was an up-and-coming young lawyer." Mary Ellen smiled. "From what I heard, she had plenty of money."

"If you hear about a relationship involving Tina, will you call me?"

"I will. Thank you for coming."

I caught up with Jack and Eddie at the freshwater pool. Eddie was having the time of his life. The water was a moderate temperature, much warmer than the ocean, and he seemed to have a natural bent toward swimming. With Jack's hand barely supporting him, he thrashed around and paddled, giggling away. I did several laps myself before relieving Jack so he could get a swim.

"Looks like you're having a good time, little one," I said to my son. "Am I going to have to buy you an Olym-pic pool when we get home?"

He babbled a little, and I convinced myself he was say-ing "pool" so I repeated it a couple of times. We bounced together in the water, getting deeper each time, and finally

I ducked us both. Eddie came up with closed eyes and a deep breath, but he didn't mind going under water. I was thrilled to have produced a natural swimmer.

When we got home, I took out one of Max Margulies's two tricycles and the one two-wheeler. The tricycle was an easy way to get around the island and there was a basket in the front that Eddie could fit into easily. I had located the property of the house that had burned down in the Eighties or late Seventies, and we cycled over. Jack wouldn't consider riding what he thought of as an old man's bike, but I was happy for the stability it provided, considering my precious cargo.

The house was different from those around it, more modern, I thought, which was not surprising, but the trees had already grown to the stature of neighboring ones.

"Look at the trim around the door," Jack said. He had dismounted and was walking around.

"The old chimney!" In an arch starting at the deck, a row of old bricks encircled the top of the door, with a few extras above for decoration. And below each of the windows, old bricks were set in a line.

The screen door opened and a man in shorts came out. He said, "Hi. Looking for something?"

"We're Chris and Jack Brooks, and Eddie, just looking at your brick trim."

"Nice to meet you. We salvaged those bricks from the old chimney of the house that used to stand here. The house was completely destroyed in a fire. We wanted to build around the chimney but we couldn't fit it into our plans. So we saved the brick."

"It's very nice. You did a great job."

"My wife and I like old things. I think it gives character to the house. We spent a lot of time scrubbing black soot off them."

"Anyone hurt in that fire?" Jack asked.

"I don't think so. The couple that owned the house said it started in the kitchen. By the time the firemen got here, the fire had gone through the roof. You see the fire yesterday?"

"We walked over. They saved most of that one."

"Yeah, but someone died, the fire chief."

I was surprised he hadn't heard about the real cause of Ken Buckley's death. "I'm glad you saved the bricks," I said.

"Me, too. Nice talking to you."

6

We had invited the Jorgensens to dinner, and I was glad Eddie had worn himself out swimming. After dinner and his bath, he was eager to go to sleep. Jack was taking responsibility for the meal, so I set up the dining room table and got the living room in order before they came.

They arrived with a bottle of red wine that they had brought from their mainland home. If I know little about cooking, I know less about wine, but Jack, who has been learning, was very impressed. He and Al discussed the merits of opening the bottle and "letting it breathe" while I put Jack's great shrimp appetizer on the table. He had decided we would eat in stages, that he wouldn't begin to grill the meat till we had finished the first course.

We ate in a leisurely fashion and talked a lot. The Jorgensens had heard that the county sheriff's department had questioned people living all around the Buckley house, a standard procedure after a homicide. The houses were fairly close together and the police hoped that someone had seen or heard something that might lead them to a suspect. But this was Fire Island and yesterday had been Labor Day and the party was on and the ocean was warm. One neighbor had seen Ken Buckley jogging toward his house, but the neighbor had been on his way

47

to the beach and hadn't been wearing a watch so he couldn't pinpoint the time.

"So it sounds as if they have nothing," Marti said.

"No one heard a shot?" I asked.

"Doesn't seem so."

"I guess the killer could have been waiting in the house," I said. "Eve Buckley said she'd been in and out all day, preparing for the party. I suppose she had to deliver the food and help set it up. Do you know if the Buckley children were on the island?"

"I think they left for college last week," Marti said. "They were here for a while earlier in the summer and got bored. I'm afraid it's what happens when they get to be teenagers. It isn't fun anymore dipping in the ocean and being with your parents."

Having spent half my adolescence in a convent, it wasn't anything I could vouch for firsthand. "And I wouldn't be surprised if the Buckleys left their door unlocked."

"Lots of folks do," Al said. "Especially when you're running back and forth all day. It's really a very safe community. Or it was until yesterday."

We talked some more and then we went outside, where Jack's grill was ready to go. Marti started to talk to him about his marinade and I went over to Al, who was standing facing the ocean. Off to our right sunset was ending with a trace of reds and oranges and pinks.

"You see it every day of your life and you never get tired of it," Al said. He was a big man who smoked a cigar after dinner and enjoyed stretching out on the sand, but rarely went into the water.

"It looks better somehow over the ocean. Nothing gets in the way."

"Marti said you wanted to talk to me. Shall we walk on the beach?"

"Let's."

We both took off the sandals we were wearing and left them on the deck. Marti seemed to understand what was going on and she stayed with Jack. I could hear her voice as we walked away.

"I'm interested in Ken Buckley's murder," I began. "Part of the reason is that I saw a girl from the Kleins' house leaving the area with soot on her face. She was covering herself with a fireman's turnout coat and later she denied having spoken to me."

"So Marti said. Suspicious behavior. And a blow to your credibility."

"Yes."

"And you'd like to ask me what I was alluding to the other night when Marti stopped me from blabbing."

"If you wouldn't mind telling me."

"I don't mind at all," Al said. We passed a couple walking in the opposite direction and Al exchanged hellos with them. "Buckley became involved with the daughter of a friend of mine a couple of years ago. She was old enough to do as she pleased, but her parents were pretty shaken up by it."

"Because he was older and married and everyone in the community knew him?"

"Those are three good reasons. I don't think they wanted him involved with her under any circumstances, even if he had been a single man, but to have a philandering fool taking up with their daughter was more than they could handle."

"What happened?"

"It wasn't pretty. First the inevitable happened." He paused.

"She got pregnant," I said.

"Not surprisingly. The summer was over by then and

everyone had gone home. There was a major confrontation between my friend and Ken. I have to tell you, it took a while to set up. Ken is very adept at avoiding confrontations, especially when he's living miles away from his accuser. He makes appointments and doesn't show. My friend had to threaten to camp on his doorstep before Ken finally kept an appointment."

"It sounds dreadful."

"It was. There was never any question of Ken leaving Eve and marrying the girl. I don't think anyone wanted that. By that time the girl wanted to be done with him. What my friend wanted was for Ken to own up and pay up."

"And did he?"

"He owned up. And he paid a little something, not as much as they agreed to."

"Then the girl had an abortion."

"It was the only way."

I didn't argue. "And the father still carries a grudge."

"Do you blame him?"

"I don't. I'm just thinking about where grudges lead."

"Not to murder, at least not in this case. My friend sold his house in Blue Harbor and moved to another town on Fire Island. He'd been planning to do it anyway and this gave him the impetus. His daughter is now happily married and it's all behind them."

It sounded like a neat wrapping-up of a sordid affair. "When did this happen?" I asked.

"Oh, must be four years by now. Maybe five. I haven't kept track."

"Do you know the Buckleys, Al?"

"I know a lot of people. We're certainly not friends."

"I understand that. I just wondered if you had any insight on why Eve has stayed with Ken all these years."

"The simplest answer is, she got something from the marriage. They have two nice kids, a beautiful house somewhere, and Ken made a lot of money. Maybe those are three reasons."

"Maybe."

We both stopped walking at the same moment. We had left Blue Harbor and crossed into the beach of the next town. We turned away from where the sun had set and started walking back.

"There's something else," Al said. "I heard Eve and Ken had decided to try to turn their marriage around."

"You mean Ken had decided."

"And Eve agreed to work on it. There was someone he was interested in at the beginning of the summer, a young, dark-haired lawyer. Good-looking woman. There are several stories making the rounds, but the one I heard was that he told her he was going back to his wife and she left Fire Island and hasn't been seen since."

I didn't think a dark-haired lawyer in her thirties could be mistaken for Tina Frisch. But before I could say anything, Al stopped and looked up at the dune. An almost invisible figure sat up there, the tip of a cigarette glowing.

"Evening, Chief," Al called.

"Who's that?" a familiar voice called back.

"Al Jorgensen. Walking with Chris Brooks."

"Nice to see you. Have a good evening, folks."

We waved and sent our greetings and then I said, "Is that Chief La Coste?"

"One and the same. He sits out there every night, smokes a cigarette—or two—and contemplates the eternal verities."

I smiled. I had seen the glow on the dune one night last week when I took a stroll along the beach.

"We were talking about the beautiful young lawyer," Al said.

"And that Ken had gone back to his wife. Then someone shoots him. It doesn't sound as though his wife did it."

"His wife? You didn't think Eve could have done this, did you?"

"I think she's one of many possible suspects. I've never come across so many people with a motive to kill one man. It doesn't mean they all had murder in their hearts, but it wouldn't surprise me if at least one of them did. What do you think, Al? We know Ken was shot. Who's your favorite to be the killer?"

"I hadn't thought about it. I guess I assumed someone had gotten off the ferry looking for an empty house to rob."

"Seems like a lot of trouble to go to just to rob a house. First you park your car in Bay Shore, then you get on a ferry, then you find the right house. And if you're spotted, where do you go? You're on an island."

Al laughed. "I guess that shows why I'm in industry and not in the business of catching crooks."

Ahead of us I could see Jack and Marti on the deck next to the grill. "I hope you're hungry," I said to Al. "Our main course should be just about ready." I waved and Marti waved back. I thanked Al for telling me what he knew and then I set it all aside for the rest of the evening.

"Did he tell you the name of his friend?" Jack asked, after I had related Al's story much later that evening.

"He didn't give a hint. Never even used his first name. It was 'my friend' over and over. I'm sure we can find out, if it comes to that. He certainly had a motive, but at this point, it's kind of weak. His daughter is happily married and she's put this all behind her. Do you wait five years to get even?"

"Who knows what people do?" Jack said. "In my experience, the most amazing things have happened. Human nature is pretty unpredictable."

"I think I'll sleep on it," I said, feeling completely done in.

"I'll call the Blue Harbor chief cop tomorrow and see if anything's turned up."

"Sounds good," I said. I was already half asleep.

The traffic pattern, if you could call it that, tended to move toward the beach most of the day and then away from it toward dinnertime. People walked in bare feet and sandals, in sneakers and rubber flip-flops, alone, in groups, in couples. Since school was starting in New York and all the suburbs, the only children walking past our kitchen window on Wednesday morning were small ones and the crowds were much thinner than the week before Labor Day.

Jack went off to talk to the officer face-to-face, rather than on the phone. When Eddie fell asleep, I wheeled him outside on the deck and took a book for myself. It was too sunny on the beach side so we sat on the side facing the street, which was west.

A few doors down across the street, I could just see the ramp to the Kleins' house through the pines, who came and who went. There was one young man who was an early riser, often heading for the beach while we were having breakfast, a shirt covering his chest and much of his trunks. I had seen him go by earlier carrying snorkeling equipment. Now he climbed up the dune, his bare feet covered with sand, his shirt wringing wet.

"Hi," he called.

"Good morning," I answered. "See anything interesting under the water?"

"Some shells. Not a lot. But the water's great. Have a good day." He waved as he passed.

I watched him go down the street, his gear dripping. As he got to the house, a woman coming from the direction of Main Street also approached. He bounded up the ramp to the front door as she made her way more slowly. There was something familiar about her and I stood and walked to the deck railing to get a better look. She was in her forties, wearing jeans and a short-sleeved white shirt. As she turned to go up the ramp to the Kleins' house, I recognized Eve Buckley.

I was absolutely certain she had told me she did not know Tina Frisch. It was possible she was visiting someone else in the house, but it seemed like too much of a coincidence. Perhaps she had decided to question Tina herself.

I moved my chair so I could see the ramp to the Kleins' house without turning. No one went in or out for a long time. Then the young man I had spoken to came out and headed for the bay. That was where the food and liquor stores were. I noticed he was wearing sneakers now and had put on dry clothes. Ten minutes passed and no one entered or left the house. Then I caught sight of Jack. I waved and he waved back and picked up his pace. He came up the ramp near the kitchen door, which was near where I was sitting.

"Before you say anything," I said, leaning over for a quick kiss and then returning to my vigil, "Eve Buckley has been inside Tina's house for about fifteen minutes."

"That's interesting."

"I want to see what happens when she comes out. I

may just follow her, run into her by accident, and see if she'll tell me what she was doing there."

"Take the bike. You can catch up to her faster."

"Good idea."

Just as I said it, both Tina and Eve came down the ramp of the Kleins' house. "There they are," I said.

"Doesn't look like they're enemies."

"No, it doesn't."

The two women stood talking for a minute as a bicyclist rang a warning bell and scooted by. Then they put their arms around each other and hugged.

"Even more interesting," Jack said.

Eve then walked slowly back toward Main Street.

"You going?"

"I don't know. What's Tina doing? She didn't go back in the house."

Tina had walked around the side of the house where I could not see her. When she appeared a minute later, she had a bicycle with her.

"I'm going," I said, and I hopped on the bike and coasted down the ramp.

Tina wasn't going very fast. The street was wood and there were occasional people on foot that had to be dodged. For a little while I thought she might be on her way to the stores at the bay, but then she took a right turn. I was confident she had no idea she was being followed. I rarely see people on bikes looking back, and here she had no traffic to worry about. I took the same turn. She was about a block ahead of me. At the next corner, she turned left, back toward the bay. She made one last turn, this time to the right, and I began to have misgivings. I had come this way myself. I followed her, slowing down in case she stopped. When she turned up a ramp, I stopped so she would not see me if she looked back.

I started pedaling slowly down the street, pausing to check the house where her bicycle was propped up next to the door. She had gone to visit Chief La Coste.

7

I rode home. I wasn't about to confront Tina and I didn't know what to say to the chief, so it seemed better to get my thoughts in order and find out what, if anything, Jack could tell me. It wasn't promising.

"Bottom line is, Springer doesn't think you saw Tina at the fire."

"Well, you've just given me the best incentive to try to figure out what's going on. She was there and I saw her, and now it looks as if she's tied up somehow, not just with Eve Buckley, but with the old chief as well."

"Makes a pretty picture. Wife and girlfriend join forces to kill husband and lover."

"But where does the chief fit in, Jack?"

"Don't ask me."

"Are you going to tell Springer?"

"I don't think he wants to hear. I'm the arrogant cop from the big city. I'm the last guy he's going to let tell him what to do."

"I'm sure you haven't been arrogant," was all I could manage to say.

"The feeling I got is that everyone around here would rather consider this a murder perpetrated by an outsider than by one of their own. So they're checking who took the ferry on Labor Day, did anyone see any strangers, that sort of thing."

"There must be strangers on every trip."

"There are. They're doing what they think is right, honey. Hey, look who's coming up our ramp."

It was Chief Curt Springer himself in shirtsleeves and riding a bike. He dismounted on the deck and came to the kitchen door just as Eddie was waking up.

"Hello again, Jack," he said cordially, as he stepped into the kitchen. "Morning, Mrs. Brooks."

I acknowledged him, poured some iced tea, and started to get Eddie's lunch together.

"Nice house you've got here. Max Margulies's, right?"

Jack told him yes, it was Max's house. Springer seemed to be making small talk in preparation to saying what he had come for. I listened until he was ready.

"I thought you folks might be interested to hear that we got the autopsy report this morning."

"Very interested," Jack said.

"There's every indication that Ken Buckley was dead before the fire. There's also no evidence of sexual activity. So it looks like Ken went home to grab a nap, left the door unlocked, and some stranger came in and popped him."

"What kind of weapon was used?" Jack asked.

"Twenty-two handgun."

A woman's gun, I thought, although men have been known to use them, too.

"What was the point of entry?" Jack asked.

"The back of the neck. He was lying on his side when we found him, facing away from the door. The shooter could have come into the bedroom without being seen and shot him as he lay in bed. He was shot close-up."

"I can't see why it was necessary to shoot him," I said. "If he was sleeping, why did the shooter bother?"

"We don't know that yet, ma'am," Springer said with

perfect courtesy. "But we'll find out. The sheriff's committed to this and so am I."

"Any leads?"

"None that we're talking about."

I assumed that meant there weren't any. "Then you're sure Tina Frisch wasn't involved." I wanted to hear him say it to me.

"We're not sure of anything right now," he said judiciously. "We know where we can reach her if we have to question her again. But there wasn't any gun in the house she's staying in and there wasn't any fireman's coat. And she says she wasn't at the scene and never saw you."

"Has the body been released to the family?" I asked.

"As far as I know. Mrs. Buckley is leaving Blue Harbor today. I think the funeral is tomorrow or the next day. I heard Ken's brother made the arrangements."

"Curt," Jack said, "it seems to be common knowledge that Ken Buckley liked the ladies."

Springer smiled in spite of himself. "And they liked him. Love is a two-way street, you know."

"But he disappointed some of them, from what I've heard. Treated his wife badly. Are you looking into anything in that area?"

"We're looking into everything. I don't think Mrs. Buckley is a viable suspect. She was at the tent on the beach where lots of folks saw her. As for the others, we're trying to find out whether any of Ken's—uh—lacy friends might have been in Blue Harbor on Monday. I want you to understand we're not out to embarrass anybody. Mrs. Buckley's a good woman and Ken was as good as they come. He earned his rank with a lot of hard work over a lot of years." It sounded like a campaign speech for a dead candidate.

"Do you know what caused the fire?" I asked.

"No sign of an accelerant, I can tell you that. Seems like something on the stove ignited."

"He was cooking something?" I asked in disbelief.

"I didn't say that, ma'am. It's possible there were papers or other combustibles near the stove and a burner was left on. You'd be surprised how many fires are started that way. I can't tell you how careful we are in our restaurant."

"Where is the bedroom in relation to the kitchen?"

"Right over it."

I was about to ask for permission to look at the crime scene when Jack said, "Do you think Chris and I could walk over and take a look at the house?"

"I don't see what purpose there is—" Springer stopped, seemingly unable to say no and unwilling to say yes.

"I'm a detective," Jack said easily. "I look at crime scenes every day of the week. Here's one in my backyard."

Springer smiled. "Sure, you can. Just don't touch anything. And be very careful where you walk for your own safety. The Blooms next door have the key. I'll call and tell them to expect you."

That seemed the end of the discussion. I had Eddie in the high chair and was spooning lunch into his eager mouth. Why Chief Springer had bothered to come over, I didn't know, unless Jack had asked specifically about the autopsy.

I waved as the men left through the kitchen door. Springer didn't know or wasn't saying who the viable suspects were. He had Ken Buckley sleeping peacefully in his bed sometime after I had spoken to him on the beach. No one had seen anything in the moments that led up to the murder, and Springer pretty much pooh-poohed the only possible lead I had uncovered. It crossed my mind that maybe he had had a grudge against Buckley himself.

Jack was back in a few minutes. I had seen the two men talking on the deck

"So what do you make of it?" he asked, as I helped Eddie drink his milk from his cup.

"Looks to me like nobody's at fault. Ken Buckley accidentally left some newspapers near the stove, forgot to turn the burner off, and as he lay sleeping, someone stole into the house, shot him in the back of the head, and the house conveniently went up in flames."

"That's about the way I read it. Want to go over and look at the crime scene?"

"Definitely. Let me ask Marti if she'll keep an eye on Eddie while he's napping. Then we can go."

Marti said she'd be delighted and I wheeled Eddie over in his stroller. There was lots of shade in one area behind the Jorgensen house and Marti got comfortable with a book while Eddie slept.

Ida Bloom walked over and unlocked the front door for us. She had not, she assured us, been home when the fire started. Along with the rest of her family, she was on the beach when the smoke was sighted.

The outside of the Buckley house was still wet, and as we approached it, I could see rivulets of water still oozing from under the shingles. The ground was wet and from what I could see under the stilts, it would be a while before the lake that had formed there would dry up or find its way into the soggy earth.

Jack and I went inside the house into a charred foyer. A rug squished underfoot. Despite the warmth and light of the summer day outside, the gloom of the fire permeated the interior. The acrid smell of burned plastic and wood was very strong. Motes of black soot hung in the air. The texture of some of the wood reminded me of alligator skin. As I looked around at the blackened furniture in the living room, I wondered if Eve Buckley would ever return to this house or if it would be torn down and replaced. Springer had told Jack that the exterior appeared to be structurally sound, but the smoke and water damage inside was depressingly great.

"Here's the kitchen," Jack said, and I followed him to the doorway. Whatever color the stove and refrigerator had been before the fire, they were black now. A film of black also covered the remaining windows over the sink. One window was gone and boarded up. But the worst damage had been done to the ceiling above. The fire had burned through to the upstairs master bedroom and pieces of furniture had fallen into the kitchen. What looked like a night table had dropped directly onto the stove, where it had fueled the fire.

I had never been in a fire-ravaged home before and the enormity of the loss stunned me. Somehow seeing one room cascading into another was almost more than I could stand. I began to think of the work that would have to go into cleaning up the mess, the moving and scrubbing, the rebuilding and the inevitable replacing of possessions, some of them surely precious.

"You OK?"

"It's terrible," I said.

"I know." He walked gingerly into the kitchen and looked around. "No smell of accelerant and no flow pattern of the kind you almost always find in fires where an accelerant is used."

"Springer said there wasn't any."

"I wonder what an analysis of the wood debris would show."

"Is the floor stable?"

"Seems to be. The flames must have shot upward. It's pretty clear the stove is the point of ignition. The area acted like a chimney, with the fire moving up to the second floor. Glad I took that undergraduate course in fire science."

I backed out. "Think we can get upstairs?"

"If the stairs are there. Let's give it a try."

The stairs were almost intact. Jack went first, testing each step.

"The firemen really managed to keep the fire local," I said. "I bet they'll be able to rebuild. It looks like a nice house."

"Very nice."

At the top of the stairs Jack turned and called back for me to wait. I walked up to the top and watched him go inside a room, the doorway of which was blackened.

"You can't get too far in," he called. "The floor's gone in the middle and the ceiling's a black hole."

I went to the door. If the kitchen was terrible, this was a calamity, a calamity I felt was very close to me. A bedroom is so personal, so intimate. I could see the charred mattress and pillow, what was left of the flowered sheets Mrs. Buckley had probably chosen with care for her summer home. Nothing had escaped the wrath of the fire here. I thought fleetingly of how sometimes it was difficult to get a fire started in our fireplace. Here, apparently, there had been no impediments. Everything had burned.

I looked up and saw the sky. The fire had burned through the ceiling and through the roof above the narrow crawl space. I remembered seeing the smoke, first from a distance, then from down the narrow street. It had been pouring out of this hole.

Now that hole was a major source of light. One window had been boarded up. Either it had exploded from the pressure of the heat or the firemen had smashed it to ventilate the room.

"If you were standing anywhere between the door and the bed, you'd have had a good shot at Buckley," Jack said.

"And if you were a woman he was waiting for, you could have come into the room and said, 'Keep your eyes closed, sweetheart. I've got a surprise for you,' and walked up close without his turning around."

"Hey, you're getting pretty good at this. How many guys have you thought of popping lately?"

"Not many. But it's a good scenario. And if you were a man, you could have walked upstairs in bare feet— everybody in Blue Harbor seems to run around without shoes—and gotten in silently."

"Then you go downstairs, turn on the stove—"

"You turned it on before you went up," I said. "So the burner would be hot when you got back down."

He shot me a wary glance. "I'm starting to wonder."

"Just logic," I said, trying to sound breezy. "And there were probably lots of letters and newspapers around that would catch fire quickly if the burner was glowing."

"Well, it did plenty of damage."

We started out of the bedroom. "Did Springer say anything about robbery?" I asked.

"Not a word. You think this could have been a robbery that turned into a homicide?"

"Not really. It's just that he seems to want us to believe that, and he hasn't given us anything that points to robbery."

"He doesn't want us involved. It's as simple as that. I

think we've seen what we came for. What do you want to do next?"

"Isn't it time to canvass the neighborhood? Let's see if Ida Bloom'll talk to us."

8

Ida Bloom was still home and happy to have company. In two minutes we were installed at a little table in her living room, the deck being too hot to sit on at this time of day, she assured us. A pitcher of lemonade was followed by tall glasses with ice cubes, and squares of what looked like homemade cake appeared on a glass platter.

"It looks like you were expecting company," I said, when we were seated.

"There's always somebody," she said. "I like to be prepared. What can I tell you?"

She was a woman in her fifties, I guessed, wearing beige cotton slacks and a bright orange cotton blouse. Her hair was graying and fell in soft curls that I took to be natural. A bit on the plump side, she was well proportioned and carried herself well.

We had explained our interest in the crime scene when we first knocked on her door, so I got started without wasting any time.

"The police seem to think this was a crime of opportunity," I began, "someone getting off the ferry, finding an open house, going inside to rob it, and eventually killing the only person they found at home."

"Well, if by 'the police' you mean Curt Springer, let me tell you Curt isn't the swiftest man I've ever met. He

66

gets something in his head and he can't shake it out even when you point out the facts to him."

"I think we agree with you. This looks like a case of murder followed by arson, not robbery followed by murder."

A little smile played on her lips. "And you want to know who the usual suspects are."

"Well, if you've got a list of them, I'll certainly write them down."

"I don't have a list," Mrs. Bloom said. "I've known the Buckleys for so many years, and Eve and I have gotten to know each other so well, that I know all the gossip but I can't think of who would want to kill him. Whatever you've heard about Ken Buckley, he was a good man in most ways and he's been a good friend to us."

"But he had girlfriends and I've heard that some of his relationships came to unhappy ends."

"That's true."

"And Eve stood by him through all that."

She took a deep breath. "I don't know if I should tell you this."

I could feel my body tensing.

"Would you feel more comfortable if I took myself home?" Jack asked.

"Oh, no. Sit down. There's nothing embarrassing about what I know. It's something Eve told me some time ago when she was having a very bad couple of weeks, and I've always been a sympathetic ear, as she has to me. So you may as well know. Eve and Ken were married when they were fairly young, early twenties, I think. Ken comes from money. His father's very wealthy and I don't think he wanted his son marrying Eve, who he considered just anybody. He was wrong, let me tell you. Eve is a wonderful human being. So old Mr. Buckley insisted on a pre-nuptial agreement."

"That was a long time ago for one of those," Jack said.

"Yes, it was. But lawyers have always known about these things and there have always been agreements written up for some people. I remember an older friend of my parents, marrying after his first wife died. He wanted to protect his money from his new wife's children and she didn't want to be cut off when he died. So they weren't unheard of. What Eve told me was that old Mr. Buckley was afraid she'd leave Ken and sue for a lot of money. She had to agree not to do that."

"You mean she would get nothing if they divorced?" I asked.

"If he divorced her, she would get a large settlement. If she divorced him, there would be very little."

"Then it literally paid her to stay with him."

"It did, yes. That's not to say that she stayed with him for the money. I think she really loved him and wanted a good marriage with him. Like the old nursery rhyme, 'When he was good, he was very, very good.' "

I didn't have to ask for the last line. "And if he died?"

"I guess the laws of New York State would take care of that. You can't disinherit your wife, you know. You can't leave your home to someone else. You just can't do it."

"Is Ken's father still alive?" I asked.

"I believe he is. And I don't think that prenuptial agreement was ever set aside or invalidated. I think Eve would have told me. She referred to it once or twice over the years. She hadn't forgotten that I knew."

"What about the children, Mrs. Bloom?"

"Ida," she said with a smile. "Mrs. Bloom is my mother-in-law. I'm just plain Ida. The boys. They're both in college now. They left Fire Island before Labor Day."

"Does the name Tina Frisch mean anything to you?"

Ida pursed her lips and shook her head.

"We heard Ken was involved with a woman earlier this summer, a young lawyer."

"Oh, the lawyer. That was nothing. She came to the house a couple of times. I don't think there was any hanky-panky."

"I heard she left Fire Island rather abruptly about a month ago and hasn't been back."

"She is back," Ida said. "I saw her over the weekend."

"Do you know where she was staying?"

"Let me see. It's a little house over on—" She closed her eyes. "It's probably the Goodwins' house, small, needs work, but it's fine for one person." She wrote down an address and gave it to me.

"Did you see them together over the weekend?"

"No, I saw her on the beach. At least, I think it was her. A good-looking girl with dark hair."

That was the same minimal description I had heard. "I guess there's a lot of bad information going around."

"I always notice on the late news, when someone's arrested for some terrible crime, they talk to the neighbors and some of them think he was always getting in trouble, and some of them say what a wonderful young man he was, how helpful he was with the elderly woman next door and how he painted her house for her. I know the Buckleys. They were the best neighbors anyone could have. They didn't let their boys make a lot of noise at night, they kept their property clean, they were warm and friendly. I know someone killed Ken. I don't think it was a kid off the ferry looking for a house to rob. I think it was someone who wanted to kill Ken. But I don't believe you could fill a bus with people who wanted to get rid of him. I know he wasn't faithful to his wife and I wish he had been. She's such a good person. But if you're looking at old girlfriends, you won't find a murderer. People forgive and forget. Girls know a summer romance ends on Labor Day. Especially if the boyfriend is married."

"But if there isn't a busful of suspects, there's at least one."

"Yes, there must be one."

I waited, but she seemed to have said all she intended to.

"If anything comes to me, I'll give you a call," Ida Bloom said.

I finished my lemonade and we left.

As we started away from the house, Eve Buckley and her sister came toward us. We all stopped and I made the introductions. Mary Ellen was pulling a wagon with a suitcase on it and I realized Eve was getting ready to leave Fire Island.

"Are you going home now?" I asked.

"I have to. It's time. The funeral is Friday and I have to get back for the wake. I just wanted to take a look at the house one last time." She seemed drained, the reality of what had happened finally getting to her. I didn't envy her going into that charred, waterlogged house.

"I hope things get better," I said, a little lamely.

"Thank you. Thank you for coming by yesterday. I don't know what will come of what you told me, but I appreciate your help."

"Just one thing, Eve. The police seem to think the tragedy began as a robbery. Have you found anything missing?"

"A robbery?" she said, as though it were a strange question to ask. "There's nothing to steal. This is a summer home. I don't keep jewelry here, or silver. There's no computer. We have a couple of old TVs and a lot of summer clothes. I imagine every house is like that. People don't dress up on Fire Island, they dress way down."

"That's what I would think. But if you find anything missing, would you let me know?"

"I will. Or I'll have Mary Ellen call."

We said our good-byes and the two women continued toward the house.

"So we still don't know," Jack said. "She's keeping her little visit to Tina Frisch to herself."

"I have the sense of a whole web of interconnections in this case. It's a small town and so many people know each other. Maybe Eve and Tina are involved in this together and Eve went to see her because she couldn't chance making a phone call from her sister's house. And maybe she just went to ask Tina whether she'd been at the scene of the fire and Tina convinced her I was crazy."

"Or mistaken. Could be either. They hugged outside the house, didn't they?"

"Tina could have said something kind to Eve and Eve became emotional."

"Lots of possibilities. Where to now?"

I looked at my watch. "We still have some time. Let's drop into the firehouse. I'd like to see where those coats are kept. And if they still have Ken Buckley's."

"Lead on."

We had ridden over on trike and bicycle and I was pretty familiar now with the layout of Blue Harbor. The distances were minimal and we were at the firehouse in less than five minutes. Black and purple bunting had been draped over the front of the building and the American flag was flying at half-staff. The chief was dead.

We went inside and found two older men sitting at a table drinking coffee. They introduced themselves as Fred and Joe and invited us to join them. I declined the coffee but Jack, ever the New York cop, thrives on it.

"You folks friends of Ken?" Fred, the heavier of the two men, asked.

"We met him once," Jack said. "We're interested in the circumstances of his murder."

"You're not the only ones. Who would ever want to kill Ken Buckley? There wasn't a nicer guy on the face of the earth."

"Nice in what way?" I asked.

"Good to us, I can tell you. We wouldn't have this firehouse if not for Ken. He knew where to go for money, how to build without making taxes go sky-high. This is a second home for almost everybody on the island. No one wants to be taxed out of his mind on a second home. So to get all this and hardly have to pay for it, that's really something. Plus he donated a generous piece of change himself."

"For the firehouse?"

"So we could have this nice extra space for ourselves right here. So we could have a decent refrigerator, a nice stove, a pool table." Fred moved his hand in an arc, showing us all the amenities.

"Did all the firemen feel that way about him?" I asked.

The two men exchanged glances. "Let me put it to you this way," the other one, Joe, said. "Fred and I are what is called inactive members. When you get to sixty, you have the option to be inactive. It's reasonable, right? Age takes its toll. You can't expect a man of sixty-five or seventy—"

"Or ninety-two," Fred put in.

"Or ninety-two, God bless him, to breathe in smoke and carry a full-sized person down a ladder."

"But you're still part of the fire department."

"We're part of it and we love it. But there's a little what you could call tension between us."

"Between whom?"

"Between the active and the inactive members. Your

perspective changes a little when you get older. Maybe you don't want them to spend money for things that aren't necessities. Maybe you think that everything new in the world isn't necessarily good."

"Are you telling me there were inactive members that disapproved of how Ken was running the fire department?"

"He's telling you," Fred said, "that there were disagreements. You ever put thirty-five guys together and have them vote unanimously?"

I couldn't say that I had. Nor had I seen a convent of Franciscan nuns agree on very much. "Could someone in the fire department have had reason to kill him?" I was careful not to mention active or inactive.

The response was immediate and effusive. Adjectives flew like bullets. Ridiculous! Absurd! Impossible! Unthinkable! They shouted each other down to impress us with the preposterousness of what I was suggesting. A brotherhood to the end.

"Then let me ask you something else," I said. "We know he died of a gunshot wound. Why do you suppose the killer set the house on fire?"

They looked at each other again and I tried to decipher the glance. Was there something they were hiding or did they simply have no idea?

"I couldn't tell you why somebody would burn the house down," Fred said. "But what I will tell you is that Ken had a reputation in this community. He was the chief. Everybody knew he was the chief. He loved being the chief. If I had to guess, I'd say whoever killed him wanted to make him a kind of martyr, make him die the way he lived. It was symbolic, is all. And that's off the top of my head."

Jack picked up the conversation for a few minutes, mostly just being friendly. The men said nice things about

Max Margulies, who had been a fireman for about twenty years and who had also contributed generously, they wanted us to know, to the comfort of the firemen. It was too bad Max couldn't be here for the party this year, although, come to think of it, it wasn't much of a party.

When the conversation lagged, I said, "I have a question about the coats you wear when you go to a fire, the ones with the thick yellow stripes. Where are they usually kept?"

"You mean those heavy turnout coats OSHA makes us wear?" Joe said. "Right here in the firehouse. You have to leave all the turnout gear here because when there's a fire, wherever you are, you come here, grab your gear, and get on the truck."

"Where was Ken Buckley's gear on Labor Day?"

"Had to be here. With everybody else's."

"Where is it now?"

Fred shrugged. "Let's take a look."

We all got up and walked past the gleaming vehicles to the far wall. The entire wall was taken up with coat after coat hanging on a hook. Above each one was a fireman's helmet and on the wall above each helmet was a scrawled name. On the floor beneath each coat was a pair of waterproof boots. Some of the coats had a last name painted in large black letters on a thick, shiny yellow stripe.

"Here it is," he called. "Buckley. Everything's here."

I walked over to the start of the line. The gear was arranged alphabetically. Helmet, coat, and boots were in their appointed places, but no name appeared on the outside of the coat. I lifted it off the hook, surprised at the weight, wondering how the men wore these on ninety-degree days. Inside the collar was the name: K. Buckley. I hung it up on its hook.

"What are we gonna do with that stuff?" Joe said.

"I don't know. Maybe Mrs. Buckley wants it. As a memento."

"Yeah," Joe said. "And maybe she doesn't."

9

Marti had said not to hurry back, that she loved babies and would enjoy playing with Eddie. We sat on our bikes in front of the firehouse while I calculated distances.

"You still game for one last visit?"

"Sure. Why not? I love to listen to your interrogations. You're damn good."

I could feel myself flushing with pleasure. It was a compliment from a pro. "Thank you."

"Unsolicited and heartfelt. Where are we going?"

"I've got two ideas, Chief La Coste and the mysterious lady lawyer staying at the Goodwins' house."

"Well, Chief La Coste is an old man and I'll bet he likes his after-lunch nap."

"You're right. Let's visit the lawyer."

Like everything else in Blue Harbor, she was a few blocks from where we were. Here some of the houses were not on stilts, probably because there was better drainage or a lower water table. The house Ida had sent us to was on the shabby side, needing at the very least a good coat of paint. There were window boxes along the front but all that was growing out of them was weeds.

"I hope she got a deal on this place," Jack said, as we stopped.

"We can't all stay in Max Margulies's house. Ready?"

"I tell you what. I'm going to leave this one to you.

She's a lawyer, I'm a cop. I don't want to get entangled in something that might compromise the case if it ever gets to court."

"OK. See you at home?"

"Or somewhere. I'll leave you a note." He put his hand in his pocket and pulled out a keyring. "I've got the extra key."

I walked up to the front door and rang the bell. I heard it sound inside but I heard nothing else. I pressed it again, holding it a little longer, and waited. Then I heard something.

The door opened, and an attractive, dark-haired woman with a terrific figure said, "Hi."

"Hi. I'm Chris Bennett. I'm spending a couple of weeks here and I wanted to talk to you about something."

"Come in."

"I'm afraid I don't know your name," I said, following her into the living room. Windows were open on two sides and there was a pleasant breeze.

She said, "Sit," and took a chair for herself. She was wearing black shorts and a white sleeveless blouse and her skin was a beautiful shade of tan. "If you don't know my name, how do you know you want to talk to me?"

"It's about Ken Buckley's death."

"I see."

Well, I thought, she's a lawyer and she's only going to answer the questions I ask, till I ask something she can't or doesn't want to answer. She's not giving any more than she has to. "I understand you knew him."

"That's right."

I took a deep breath. "There are whispers around that you had a relationship with him."

She smiled. "Yes, that's true. We had a relationship, but not the kind you're hinting at. That's scurrilous gossip.

Our relationship was all business. And may I ask what your relationship to Ken Buckley was?"

"It was barely that of an acquaintance," I admitted. "It's just that there are some strange things about his death and I'm looking for answers."

"How so?"

"I saw someone at the scene of the fire. I believe she came out of the Buckley house. I told this to the police and they questioned her, but she denied having been there and even denied having seen me. It's become a matter of my integrity."

"And what do I have to do with this person and that murder?"

"That's what I'm here to find out."

She tossed her hair in a way that I was sure she did often. "I think you're going to leave disappointed, then. I know nothing about the murder and even less about the woman you saw."

"Would you mind telling me your name?" I asked.

"I'm Dodie Murchison." She got up and left the room briefly, returning with a business card.

I looked down at it. It read, "Dodie Murchison, Attorney-at-Law" and gave an address in Manhattan. "Can you tell me what your business was?" I asked, with little hope of an answer.

"I really can't. It's privileged."

"He's dead now."

"I'm sorry."

"I'm told you came out here regularly till the end of July and then you stopped coming."

"That's true. You can't always plan your life as perfectly as you'd like to. I had hoped for an easier summer but I wasn't able to get out here in August until last Friday."

"Did it have anything to do with Ken Buckley?"

"Nothing."

I was suddenly rather glad that Jack had decided not to be present. This was an embarrassingly lean conversation. Her responses were very short and gave me almost no information at all. About all I'd learned since sitting down was her name. "Do you have any idea who might have wanted Ken Buckley dead?"

She appeared to give it some thought. "I don't think I can answer that," she said. "I really never met anyone else who knew him."

"How did you meet him?"

"You might say I was in the right place at the right time."

"The beach at Blue Harbor?"

She smiled but said nothing.

"Did you ever meet Mrs. Buckley?"

"I saw her, but I don't think we ever spoke."

"I'm told you visited him at his house."

"That's true. I went there on a couple of occasions."

"Was Mrs. Buckley home?"

"You *are* persistent. I don't know if she was home. I didn't see her."

I didn't know where to go from there. If Buckley had told her something I could use, she would probably consider it privileged information.

I wrote down my name, my two addresses and phone numbers, and handed the slip of paper to her. "If you think of anything, I'd really like to hear about it."

She looked at the paper. "I'll tell you one thing. I don't think he was killed for anything that happened this summer. I think he was a man haunted by something in his past."

"Do you know what that something is?"

"I really don't think I can answer that question."

I stood. "Thank you, anyway." I looked at her card and

as I tucked it in my purse a question occurred to me. "What kind of law do you practice?"

She suddenly looked uncomfortable. For some reason, she seemed not to want to tell me but she must have known that if I had her card, all it would take was a telephone call to find the answer.

"I'm in estate planning," she said.

I cycled home as fast as I could on the uneven pavement and boards. I put the trike away and went next door where Eddie was sitting in Marti's lap. He didn't look entirely happy.

As he saw me, he said, "Ma!" loudly and reached his arms out for me.

"Well, someone's starting to talk," Marti said, handing my little son to me.

"Hi," I said to her. "Yes, I'm Mama, Eddie, and I'm home. Did you have a good time with Marti?"

"He's a bit cranky. I don't know if he missed you or if he's teething. I think he's got a little white showing on his gum."

"That's probably it," I said. I thanked her and patted Eddie's back. He had been teething on and off for months and I admitted readily that I had no idea how to deal with a cranky baby, although now that he was on my shoulder, he was quietly sucking his fingers.

Jack had left a note that he was taking a swim and I got Eddie and me both in our bathing suits and walked out on the beach, which was pleasantly empty. Jack had set up the umbrella and was just getting out of the water.

"Boy, do I love it," he said, as he got to us. "How're you doin', Eddie? Want a dip in the ocean?"

Eddie went to him readily and I followed. When we were all thoroughly wet, I said, "Her name is Dodie Murchison and she says her relationship with Ken Buckley was strictly business. She's an estate lawyer."

"I love it," Jack said. "He was changing his will."

"Sounds like it, if she's telling the truth. It was like pulling teeth getting her to say anything besides 'That's true' and 'That's privileged.' "

"I guess you were talking to a lawyer. I was thinking of practicing talking like that to you. How long would our marriage last?"

"Don't even think about it. I wait all day for you to come home and then when I ask how your day was you'll say that's privileged?"

Jack laughed. "She give anything at all up?"

"One parting line that was very intriguing. She thinks that whoever killed Ken Buckley wasn't doing it because of anything that happened this summer. She said he was a man haunted by the past."

"Aha."

"And I know she didn't want to tell me what kind of law she practiced, but she'd already handed me her card, so she couldn't keep it a secret."

"Nice work. Let's think about this. You can't change a pre-nup without both parties' agreement. So unless Eve was in on it, it wasn't the pre-nup this Dodie was working on. You have any sense of why he went to her?"

"Frankly, I think he saw her on the beach, looked at those long, gorgeous legs and that very attractive face, and started up a conversation."

"That had nothing to do with law."

"That had everything to do with her looks. She said that any gossip to the effect that she'd had an intimate relationship with him was scurrilous."

"So maybe they started talking and when she said she was an estate lawyer, he decided to talk to her about changing his will. It would give him the opportunity to have some quality private time with her and maybe he'd get the will changed without his regular lawyer knowing anything about it."

"That's probably the way it went. And then she let him know she wasn't available sexually."

"That assumes she told you the truth," my ever-skeptical husband said.

Eddie was having a great time in the water. He was splashing around and giggling, but I always worried about the sun.

"Maybe we should take some time out under the umbrella," I suggested.

We made our way out of the water and across the hot sand.

"Let's think about Tina Frisch for a second," Jack said. He picked up a towel and wrapped Eddie in it, then set him down on our big towel in the shade of the umbrella. "You think she's twenty-five?"

"Approximately. You know I'm no good at ages."

"I think she could be younger. Do we know how old Buckley was?"

"Ida said they had married young, early twenties. Their kids are in college. So add twenty years or so to the marriage age."

"Midforties. That's about what we figured. Tina could be his daughter by another woman."

"And he wanted to provide for her. That makes sense. Then the incident that Dodie Murchison said haunted him would be his relationship with another woman."

Jack looked around. "I need a piece of paper."

I laughed. He had a special way of taking notes, folding the sheet into quarters and filling one surface before refolding it and using another. "You mean you came to the beach unprepared to take notes?"

"I'm slipping. Don't tell my lieutenant. OK, that's one

good option. It doesn't explain what Tina's relationship is to old Chief La Coste."

"It may be very benign," I said. "He told me that people came in and helped him out, you know, cooked for him, made him lemonade, maybe cleaned up the house. She may be a good samaritan."

"Who had some relationship to Buckley. Damn. I wish I had a piece of paper." But he made no move to get up and leave.

It was so pleasant here, the breeze from the water so relaxing, I had no desire to move. Ever. "Maybe she just happened to go to his house to talk to him on Labor Day. And found him dead in his bed."

"With a fireman's coat? So she set the house on fire?"

"Stranger things have happened in real life."

"Try telling that to a district attorney."

"Jack, if Tina was going to benefit from a change in Ken Buckley's will, it's not very likely she killed him. Or that she set his house on fire."

"Did this Murchison woman give you any idea of whether their business had been concluded?"

"None. How long does it take to change a will?"

"Not long. You get together with your attorney, decide what you want, and the new will is typed up. Or a codicil is added. He could have left the original will intact and added on a clause that said that in addition to all the other bequests, he wanted so-and-so to receive such-and-such an amount of money. Or real estate. Or jewelry. Or whatever. It doesn't have to change the main part of the will. If he said in the will that after the bequests were made the remainder of the estate was to be divided among his wife and sons, then one additional bequest just diminishes the amount to be divided. He doesn't know on any particular day how much he's worth. None of us do. You own a hundred shares of AT&T and it goes up and down. At some point in the will you have to refer to the rest or the remainder after specific bequests have been paid."

"And the prenuptial agreement is invalid if he dies."

"I can't say that, but if what Ida said is true, he was afraid of Eve leaving him and suing for a lot of money. If she stuck around till he died, that was proof of her fidelity."

"It's also a motive for murder."

"Obviously."

"Maybe the pre-nup was what haunted him," I said. "Maybe he regretted his father's pushing him to get it."

"Then Eve would have to agree to a change. They both signed it."

"It's an embarrassing thing to ask her."

"Maybe Murchison will tell you if you let her know you know about the pre-nup."

"Right."

We both lay down with Eddie between us. This was the life. I closed my eyes, trying to think of what else might have been haunting Ken Buckley. I rather hoped he wanted to invalidate the prenuptial agreement, make his wife an equal partner. It seemed very cruel of him to have imposed conditions on their marriage. But I supposed if the money involved had been his father's, as it must have been, he probably hadn't had much of a choice. I tried to imagine how I would have felt if Jack had said that he loved me and wanted to marry me but there was a little matter of protecting his assets. From me. I was older than Eve at marriage; I had reached my thirty-first birthday. Still, such a proposition would have stung me deeply. I didn't know enough about wealthy people to know whether such an agreement was the usual thing, particularly twenty-plus years ago.

I found myself feeling very sorry for Eve. Two decades of marriage and he still didn't trust her motives. She had borne and raised their two sons, stuck with him when many other women would have given up. Had it all become too much to bear? Had she seen him with the beautiful Dodie Murchison and assumed the worst when, in fact, her husband was righting an old wrong?

How long would it have taken for Eve to dash back to her house on Labor Day, leave the magnificent picnic for just a few minutes, and shoot him once in the back of the head? I couldn't believe she would have been missed. There had been many women at the tent, several of them moving around, making them hard to keep track of.

It was a possibility. I breathed deeply. In a few minutes, I was fast asleep.

10

There was no way I could talk to Eve for several days. She had returned to her home for the wake and funeral, and common courtesy dictated that she not be disturbed during this period of mourning. I would have to look elsewhere for information.

While I might understand Eve being driven to murder by the combination of a prenuptial agreement that virtually kept her a prisoner in her marriage and a philandering husband who abused her love, I really couldn't imagine her setting fire to her own house, unless the house itself represented something ugly in her marriage. Perhaps she had wanted to vacation in Maine or Arizona or Paris and Ken wanted only to go to Fire Island, where he enjoyed being fire chief. Marriages, I have discovered, are strange relationships, iceberglike, with the great bulk out of sight.

Eve's sister called to answer my question around dinner time.

"Eve wanted me to tell you," Mary Ellen said, "that she looked around as best she could and as far as she could see, nothing was missing."

"I appreciate your call. If nothing is missing, that certainly tells me it wasn't robbery."

"Did you really ever seriously consider that it was? A man lying in bed shot in the back of the head? It sounds like revenge to me."

"Revenge for what?"

"I don't have the slightest idea. Ken had a top position in his family's business. Although I believe he was well liked, he could have angered any number of people."

"Mary Ellen, when you and I talked yesterday, you told me that Ken had been involved with a young lawyer this summer."

"And that she left Fire Island the beginning of August."

"She's in Blue Harbor right now."

"She is?" The surprise in her voice sounded genuine.

"I saw her. She came for the Labor Day weekend and she's staying—I don't really know until when."

"I'm surprised to hear that. I had a conversation with her myself the first weekend in August, after which she didn't come back."

"You talked to her?"

"I told her to leave my sister's husband alone. It may not have been my business, but sometimes these things just get to be too much. I didn't seek her out. I saw her and said my piece. When she didn't come back, I thought that was the end."

"I talked to her myself this afternoon. She said any rumors that she was having an intimate relationship with Ken were scurrilous. She said she was doing business with him. I assumed it was legal business. She's an estate attorney."

"Wills and things like that?"

"Yes."

"Well, that's ridiculous. Ken has every kind of attorney you could ever want. He doesn't need to find one on the beach at Blue Harbor." There was a derisive tone to her voice that told me how she felt more than her words did.

"Mary Ellen, I know that Eve signed a prenuptial agreement. Do you know if it was still in effect when Ken died?"

I heard her sigh. "She's never told me they got rid of it."

"Perhaps this lawyer, Dodie Murchison, was working on a new agreement that would eliminate the pre-nup. Maybe Ken didn't want to deal with his regular lawyer on this to make sure it was kept private."

"Lawyers aren't supposed to talk about their clients' business."

"Maybe Ken felt something would get back to his father."

"I see what you mean. Anything is possible, of course, but I'm convinced there was more than legal business going on between them."

It occurred to me that we might both be right. Dodie could have been doing business with Ken and sleeping with him besides. "Perhaps that's true," I said. "I'd like to ask you one other thing. Did something happen in Ken's life, perhaps a number of years ago, that might have burdened his conscience?"

She gave a quick laugh. "He cheated on my sister. It *should* have burdened his conscience."

"What I mean is, could he have hurt someone else, outside his family, in such a way that he might have wanted to make amends?"

"You're looking for someone he might have wanted to pay back."

"Yes."

"Well, I can see why he wouldn't go to the family lawyer in a case like that. Offhand, I can't think who that might be. Eve and I are close, but no one bares her deepest secrets, even to a sister. And if I don't know, I don't know who would."

"One more thing. Does Eve like her house in Blue Harbor? Does she enjoy coming out here?"

"Interesting that you should ask that. Ken was the one who really loved Fire Island. I don't mean to say that Eve disliked it. She has lots of friends here and my husband and I are here. She and Ken always took a winter vacation to some wonderful, warm place. But I think she would have preferred spending less time here and more time somewhere else. She mentioned Hawaii to me. She felt she hadn't seen enough of Europe. She wanted to visit Hong Kong."

So there might have been a motive to burn down the house. I thanked Mary Ellen and asked her to keep me informed in case anything turned up.

I talked to Jack about it while we had coffee on the deck facing the ocean.

"Your good-looking lawyer may have intentionally pointed you in the wrong direction by mentioning Buckley's past indiscretions. To keep you from looking in the here-and-now."

"That's what occurred to me as Mary Ellen was talking. But you know, I just can't quite see Dodie Murchison shooting Ken Buckley. She's a young woman, an up-and-coming lawyer. There'd have to be a lot more at stake than a failed summer romance to risk a stiff jail sentence at the very least."

"Maybe there was."

"I think I should talk to her again, Jack." I looked at my watch. "Now that I've heard what Mary Ellen Tyler has to say, I'll be in a position of greater strength."

"Go to it. I don't mind getting back to my reading. Next week's the beginning of the semester."

And the end, I thought, of finding all the suspects conveniently assembled in a small area between the ocean and the bay. When the weekend came, they would all be returning to their permanent homes in and around New York City. "There are two other people I want to talk to," I told him, "although they'll probably have to wait till tomorrow. If I'm to find out what Buckley's past transgressions were, Chief La Coste might know. He seems to know everything that's happened in this town. And how about Curt Springer?"

"He'll know if Buckley got into trouble and he was called. There may not be a paper trail on those incidents, though. These guys are good to each other. Someone calls up and says Buckley's been drinking too much and is making an ass of himself and Springer comes along, calms everybody down, and gets Buckley home safely. No report, therefore it never happened. And even if there is paper, he may not show it to you."

None of this surprised me. To some degree, it didn't even bother me. Should there be a police report because a man drank too much and was loud? It wasn't as if he hurt anyone, broke anything, or was planning to get in a car and drive somewhere. But it made my job more difficult.

"Springer may not be very well disposed to me, anyway," I said. "I sounded pretty incredulous when he said he thought the motive was burglary."

"I'm sure you're not the only one with that reaction."

I finished my coffee and gathered the dishes together. "Let me get a shirt to put on. It's getting cool. I'll take the bike."

"You OK at night?"

I smiled. "You mean, do I think someone got off the ferry half an hour ago and is looking for a young mother without a dollar on her to rob? I'll be fine."

I took a quick swing by Chief La Coste's house. There was only one light on in the section where the bedrooms were so I kept going. Dodie Murchison's house had lights on in several rooms. I rang the bell.

"Chris Bennett," she said, when she recognized me. "Find your killer yet?"

"Not yet, but I have a couple of questions."

"Come in. I'm having a glass of brandy," she said, as we went into the living room. "Join me?"

"I don't think so, thanks." I sat in a different chair from that afternoon. "I got a call from Mrs. Buckley's sister a little while ago." I wanted her to know I hadn't initiated the conversation. "She said she talked to you about a month ago."

"The Tyler woman? That conversation was like a bad soap opera. She accused me of having an affair with Ken and told me to stay away from her sister's husband. It was rather childish."

"I think she cares a great deal for her sister and didn't want to see her hurt."

"I wasn't hurting her. I told you, my business with Ken Buckley was business."

"I thought maybe that was the reason you didn't come out here during August."

"I was busy at work in August."

"Did you see him during the Labor Day weekend?"

"I may have. I saw a lot of people over the weekend."

"A few years ago, Ken had a summer romance with a girl who became pregnant. Did you know about that?"

"Ken never told me. I didn't know."

"I thought perhaps he wanted to make some kind of gift or bequest to her to apologize for rather boorish behavior on his part."

"Boorish? Did he insist on an abortion when she got pregnant?"

"They both wanted an abortion. He ducked paying for it."

"Well, I can't help you. I know nothing about that, and anyway, women should insist on protection if they have casual sex."

"I mention this because of what you said this afternoon, that Ken was haunted by something that happened in his past. I thought that might have been the incident."

"If it was, he didn't tell me about it."

"Did he tell you anything that might lead to his killer?" She took a sip of the brandy and rolled the snifter between her palms. "Chris, I would like to help you but I can't. I don't like the idea of a killer going free any more than you do. But what I learned from Ken is privileged and even if I told you what I know, I don't know if it would help find his killer."

"Ken and his wife signed a prenuptial agreement before they were married. Do you know if it's still in effect?"

That stopped her. "How do you know about that?"

"Eve talked about it. Someone told me."

"To my knowledge it was in existence at the time of his death."

"Then he told you about it."

"We discussed it, yes."

"Did Ken sign any agreement that you prepared before he died?"

"He signed nothing."

"Do you have something with you that he would have signed if he had lived?"

"You're making this very difficult for me. We discussed something early in the summer. Ken died before any papers could be executed. I have no intention of carrying this discussion any further. These things happen. Without a signature, what he said to me is not legally binding. I'm not sending the family a bill for my services. It never happened."

I thanked her and started for the door.

"I have a question," she called after me.

I turned.

"The girl you saw running from the Buckley house during the fire. Do you know her name?"

"Tina Frisch."

"She's a grouper?"

"Yes. She's living in the Kleins' house, across from ours. It's near the ocean."

"Thank you."

I left. Whatever Ken Buckley had meant to do, his killer had put an end to his intentions, good or bad. Perhaps that's exactly what the killer meant to do.

11

I started Thursday by watering the boxes of fresh herbs that lined the sunny sides of the deck. The Margulieses grew many varieties, all well labeled, and Jack had been using them in his cooking, commenting that next summer we would have to grow our own.

When everything was damp to the touch, I cycled to the little police station near the bay. It was part of the substantial building that included the firehouse and, in a small wing, housed all the municipal offices of Blue Harbor. The latter didn't take up a lot of rooms or require very much space. One secretary manned all the telephones and didn't seem overwhelmed with work. She told me Chief Springer was on the phone but I could go in as soon as he was off.

It didn't take long. The secretary glanced at her phone, buzzed him, and told him Mrs. Brooks was waiting to see him. He allowed me to cool my heels long enough to impress me with his importance and then opened his door and ushered me in.

"Something I can do for you?" he asked cordially.

"I'm still thinking about Ken Buckley's murder," I said. "I've learned a few things about Ken in the last two days."

"Anything I should know?"

"Probably things you already know," I admitted. "Did he have any kind of criminal record here in Blue Harbor?"

"Criminal record? Not as long as I've been here."

"Have there been complaints about him? Were you ever called to settle any differences he was involved in?"

He narrowed his eyes. "Where are you going with this, Mrs. Brooks? You have something particular in mind?"

"I wondered if he might have angered someone in town, if someone could have built up a great resentment against him."

"For what?"

"That's really what I'm asking you."

"If you're referring to the night he and a couple of firemen took the fireboat for a personal ride, I don't think that built up any resentment. They were all given a dressing-down and that was the end of it."

"Was there any damage to the boat?"

"Not officially."

"Then he's been involved in situations that didn't get written up."

Springer smiled. "Everyone has, ma'am. Haven't you ever been stopped for going through a red light and were left off with a warning? That's done all the time. The officer has a lot of discretion. He looks at you, you're a nice young woman who lives in the town; he doesn't want to upset your life. He takes a chance that if he stops you this once, you'll remember not to do it in the future, and that's the point of his stopping you in the first place."

"Tell me about the other times you saved Ken Buckley from being written up."

Springer walked to the door and closed it. As he came back to his chair, he scratched the side of his neck. He was wearing a short-sleeved shirt and the windows were open. There was an air conditioner in the wall he could have used but the breeze coming in from the bay was very pleasant. His office looked out on the bay and in the distance I could see the ferry approaching. He was both the symbol and the sole keeper of law and order in this little town. I was sure there were many nights, especially in the summer, when he was hauled out of bed to mediate a quarrel or get some injured person to a mainland hospital, and he was surely paid precious little for his time and trouble, half-time pay when he could be called any time at all.

"You don't know very much about Ken Buckley, do you?" he asked.

"Very little. I met him the day before he died, when we visited the firehouse."

"And you got interested in this case because you thought you saw that girl from the Kleins' house at the fire."

"I saw her," I said. "She had a fireman's coat over her head."

"I remember you telling me that. Well, Ken Buckley was a very spirited man," Curt Springer said. "He was very well liked, he was a great fire chief, and he sometimes went off the deep end. It's probably those situations you want to hear about."

That sounded as good a place to start as any. "I think so."

"I can tell you he loved that fireboat the way some men love their Beamers. Close your eyes and Ken Buckley was off in the fireboat. It was always business, you understand. He had to check this and fix that. The truth is, he just got a charge out of it. The night he went out with the other firemen, he was six sheets to the wind, and that's a danger."

"But there were other times."

"Yes, there were. The last time I saw him in it was near the beginning of the summer. He was with some lady who's a member of the legal profession and I let her think she convinced me not to write it up. Ken knew what was going on but it was good for her ego."

"I'm sure it was. Go on, Chief. This is all very interesting."

"There've been some calls over the years about people screaming at each other in the Buckley house."

"Mrs. Buckley was screaming?"

"I'd have to say yes."

"Did he strike her?"

"I don't think Ken ever laid a hand on anyone. These were arguments, a couple of folks mad at each other. That's all. Happens more than you'd think."

"I'm sure you have your hands full here," I said sympathetically.

"I'm not complaining. It's the best job in the world—next to owning a good restaurant. I get to live on an island and the truth is, I don't overwork myself in the winter."

"I'm sure Chief La Coste doesn't give you any trouble."

"Bernie's the greatest guy in the world. I hope he lives forever."

"I do, too." I considered what he had told me. "I don't suppose anyone ever complained about the fireboat."

"Not a word."

"Can you think of anything else? Did anything happen between Ken and Tina Frisch?"

"Not that I know of. First I heard of her was what you told me."

"And the lady lawyer. I think her name is Murchison. Anything else happen there?"

His eyebrows rose at the sound of her name. "I didn't see much of her this summer. The only time I ever met her was when I saw her out on the boat with Ken."

"You knew the Buckleys for years. What's your assessment of their marriage?"

"I don't get involved in people's lives, Mrs. Brooks. If they shouted at each other a couple of times, well, that's what life does to you. If anyone asked me to assess your marriage, what would I say? You're a nice young couple with a baby. I guess I'd give Jack the benefit of the doubt because he's a cop, but other than that, I don't know you. I just try to be fair. For all I know, you aren't even married. You just got together for the summer. People's private lives contain a lot of deep, dark secrets."

"I see what you mean. How long have you been in Blue Harbor?"

"As chief of police? They hired me thirteen years ago when I was just thirty-one. I spent a year working with the outgoing chief, Jerry O'Donnell. When he retired, I took over. He didn't stay on, by the way. He went down to Florida. Lives on Key West. Couldn't stay off an island."

"I'm sure it's in your blood."

"Are you going to Ken's funeral tomorrow?" he asked.

"I don't think so. We hardly knew him and we're leaving on Sunday. I suppose a lot of Blue Harbor people will be there."

"Oh, yes. We're all taking the same ferry tomorrow morning. The town'll be empty except for the groupers. They never get to know the homeowners. And we never get to know them very well."

All the interesting little grudges that built up in a community. The all-year-round people versus the summer folks, the renters versus the owners, the inactive firemen versus the active. It made you understand why world peace was so hard to achieve. "How long did the Buckleys live on Fire Island?" I asked.

"Longer than I've been here. They were in a smaller house when they first came. Later they moved into the present house."

"Was Ken a fireman back then?"

"I heard he became a fireman the first year they were out here. He's been chief for a number of years."

"Were you here when that house burned down? Chief La Coste said that was the biggest fire ever on the island."

"That was a year or so before I came. I remember seeing the chimney."

"Well, I guess that's it." I started to thank him for his time but the phone rang, cutting me off.

As he lifted the phone I could hear a frightened voice at the other end. "I'll be right there," he said, pushing his chair back as he spoke. "Don't touch anything." He hung up. "Sorry. I've got to go, Mrs. Brooks. There's a problem." He dashed out of the office as I stood, and by the time I got outside he was gone.

It was still only mid-morning and I thought it would be a good time to visit Chief La Coste and see what else he could tell me. If he really knew everything that went on, I could use him to confirm what I had learned from everyone else. I didn't expect him to know about Ken Buckley's intimacies but he might know that Ken had been picked up—with a woman aboard—on the fireboat. Dodie Murchison certainly conducted business in intriguing settings: on the beach, in her house and his house, and on the boat. I guessed that Eve had left Fire Island from time to time, perhaps to go shopping or see to her sons' needs or just to visit friends in her hometown, leaving the house empty. I wondered, however, why Ida Bloom poohpoohed the idea of Ken having an intimate relationship with Dodie. Ida had seemed sure there was nothing but business between them.

I biked over to the chief's little house and knocked on the door.

He came to the door, looked around, and said, "Where's the baby?"

I laughed. "I left him home with his daddy. I've been

biking around Blue Harbor talking to people. Do you have time for me?"

"I've got time for everything in my life. Come in."

We walked through the house as we had the other day, ending in the kitchen, where he took a full pitcher of lemonade out of the refrigerator and poured two glasses.

"Would you mind sitting inside today?" he asked. "It's a little breezy out this morning."

"Inside's fine."

We carried our glasses into the living room and sat down. As I looked around, a lamp caught my eye and I got up to look at it.

"You picked out my treasure," the chief said. "That's an old copper and brass fire extinguisher from maybe sixty years ago. I had it turned into a lamp more years ago than I can remember. Takes a lot of polishing but I enjoy doing it."

"It's beautiful. I can almost see myself in it. It really is a treasure."

"Lots of the older fellows have 'em. Age has its benefits—along with the aches and pains."

"You're in great shape, chief." I lingered at the old, round mahogany drum table on which the lamp stood. In a semicircle around it were framed photos in various sizes, many of them quite old. One, in a more elaborate frame, was of the chief and his bride on their wedding day. "These are wonderful pictures," I said.

He got out of his chair and came to stand beside me. "She was a beauty, my Bessie. Look at that smile. Look at that figure. See the lace on her dress? All handmade, every inch of it. My daughter wore it when she got married and it's been passed on. And on."

"It looks like a wonderful family. There must be a lot of them by now."

"Well, it's over sixty years since we said, 'I do.' That's

a lot of generations. I've got great-grandchildren growing up now."

"Any of them live on Fire Island?"

"Not a one. They're spread to the four winds."

"They're lucky to have you," I said, thinking as I always did at moments like these how much my own parents would have loved to have a son-in-law and a grandson.

He appreciated the compliment. "But it's my memory you're here for. Right?"

"Right. I've heard a lot of stories since I talked to you. I want to find out which are fiction and which are truth."

He settled back in his chair. "I guess there's a little fiction in any old story you can think of."

"Let me start with some newer stories. I'm told Ken Buckley often took the fireboat out as his own private pleasure boat."

"Well, I guess that's true enough. The fireboat didn't get much use. He probably did it a favor by taking it out. Found all the kinks before they could cause trouble."

He certainly was a loyal friend. "I understand he had company with him the last time he took the boat out."

The chief smiled. "Well now, Ken did like the ladies. That was a lawyer he had with him, did you know that? I guess Curt Springer scared the living daylights out of her. Don't look too good for lawyers when they break the law." He was enjoying the story.

"Do you know her at all?" I asked, just on the slim chance that he did.

"Well, I saw her once or twice. Good-looking lady. They didn't make lawyers like that back when I was a young man."

I didn't bother explaining that the women who might have wanted to become lawyers back then were kept out of law school by the men who were now his age and probably his son's age. "Are you going to Ken's funeral tomorrow?"

"I haven't decided yet. I'd sure like to. We were friends for a long time. It's just that it gets hard for me, even a little trip like that. I'll get up in the morning and see how I feel."

"Did you see a lot of Ken, Chief?"

"Saw him all the time. He came to visit almost every day."

"I didn't realize you were so close."

"We liked each other, plain and simple. We just talked. Anything I needed, Ken would get it for me. I miss him, you know that?"

"I can see why. Do you have a good relationship with Curt Springer, too?"

"We're friendly, but it's not the same. He's a nice fella but he doesn't hold a candle to Jerry O'Donnell. Now there was a police chief."

"You know, I keep thinking that the person who killed Ken Buckley was someone who lives on Fire Island, probably in Blue Harbor. But everyone I've talked to liked him and I haven't found anyone who had a reason to want to kill him."

"Can't think of one myself."

"Remember, I told you I saw a girl from a group that lives at the Kleins' house? A girl who was leaving the Buckley house during the fire?"

"I remember. She had a fireman's helmet or something."

"A turnout coat."

"Right. A coat. Shoulda been in the firehouse. That's where they belong."

"Her name is Tina. Tina Frisch. Do you recognize the name?"

"Doesn't ring a bell."

"I thought I saw her drop over here yesterday."

"Here? This house?"

"Yes."

"What would she do that for?"

"That's what I was wondering."

"Don't know any Tinas. There was a girl helped me out all summer, name of Mindy. They've gone home now so she can go to school."

"Who helps you now?"

"There's a family of year-rounders in the next block named Partridge, if you can believe it. They've got a little French girl working for them. She's been helping out. Makes good lemonade, what do you think?"

"It's terrific."

"Maybe that's who you saw, my little French girl, Brigitte."

"Yes, maybe so." For whatever reason, he didn't want to admit that he knew Tina and I didn't want to press it. I recalled that when we had spoken on Tuesday, he had continuously steered the conversation away from Ken Buckley's possible murderer. I didn't think for a moment it had been Chief La Coste but I felt he knew something he didn't want to tell me. Perhaps it was Tina's involvement. But I had no idea what his relationship to Tina might be. When I had looked at the photos on the drum table, I had looked for her picture, but it hadn't been there.

"Guess I haven't helped very much," the chief said, as I sat thinking.

"I've learned a lot from you and I'm very grateful."

"Well, I always enjoy the company."

I stood and waited for him to lead the way out of the living room. As he passed in front of me, the phone rang. He went to answer it and as he listened, I saw his face lose its color. He reached for a kitchen chair and sat, shaking his head. He said "Yes" a couple of times, then hung up.

"What is it?" I asked.

"There's been another murder."

"Oh, no."

"Terrible. Just terrible."

"Let me stay with you for a while."

"No. I'll just lie down for a bit. Take a nap, maybe." He got to his feet and turned toward the bedroom. "Can you find your way out?"

"Sure." I watched as he started away.

"I'm fine," he called, without looking back.

As I turned to go, I saw a row of hooks on the kitchen wall near the door to the deck. A man's straw hat hung on one hook. On the hook next to it was a fireman's turnout coat, black with yellow stripes.

12

My heart was pounding and my stomach churning all the way home. As I turned down our street, I saw a few people, mostly women, in front of the Kleins' house. I stopped one and asked what was going on.

"Someone's dead," she said. She looked very pale.

"In this house?"

"Yes. They found a body about an hour ago. No one will say anything."

"Oh, my God." I pushed the bike the rest of the way to our house and was at the top of the ramp when Jack came out from the kitchen.

"You hear what happened?" he said.

"A woman told me somebody had died in the Kleins' house. And Chief La Coste got a call just before I left."

"I think it's Tina."

"*What?*"

"I can't swear to it. Springer wouldn't let anyone near the crime scene. Someone in the house found a body in the crawl space near the back of the house. I walked over with Eddie and got as close as I could. It's a girl and there's blond hair. Sun-bleached."

"Tina's."

"That's all I could see."

"This is terrible. She's a young girl. What could she have done?"

"She could have killed Ken Buckley."

We went into the kitchen and I took Eddie from him. He looked as though he'd just woken up. He cried a little and nestled his head in the crook of my neck. I put my arms around him and held him as though I could protect him forever from the evils of the world he would grow up in.

I took him upstairs and changed him and he came fully awake and smiled when I played with him. I carried him downstairs and we all went into the living room. Eddie sat on the floor and played with some of the toys that were spread out in what had become a very baby-centered room.

Jack had two tall glasses of iced tea waiting and I took a long sip of mine when I sat down.

"You OK?" Jack said.

I nodded and took another sip. "Chief La Coste said it was murder but he didn't say who. Do you know how it happened?"

"No one's saying."

"Jack, I want to find Dodie Murchison." I got up and went to the kitchen where the telephone book was and looked up the phone number at Dodie's house. I let it ring about twenty times before I hung up.

"She's not there or she's not answering," I told Jack. I looked at my watch. "Do you mind if I dash over there? I saw her last night. I'd like to know what she's been doing with her time since I left her."

"Go 'head. We'll be fine."

"I'll be back to give Eddie his lunch." I got down on the floor and stuck my face in his face and listened to him giggle. "I'll see you soon, sweetheart," I said. I stood up and waved and he seemed to wave back. I threw a kiss and ran.

Dodie's house was locked and all the windows were closed. After I knocked and knocked, I circled the house, but she wasn't sitting outside and I couldn't see her through any of the windows.

When I got back around to the front, a woman came out of the house next door and came over to where I was getting ready to get on the bike and go home.

"She left this morning," the woman said.

"Left Blue Harbor?"

"That's what it looked like. She had a couple of suitcases on a wagon and she was walking toward the ferry."

"What time was that?" I asked.

"Pretty early. Sometime after seven."

"Was anyone with her?"

"I didn't see anyone."

"I'm Chris Bennett," I said, holding out my hand. "I'm here with my family for a couple of weeks."

"I'm Jean Hill."

"Did you get to know her?"

"Not much. We said hello. She didn't come out here that often and she kept to herself most of the time. I don't think she was here at all last month till Labor Day weekend. I have the Goodwins' extra key and I keep my eye on the house for them."

"Did anyone come to visit her?"

"I couldn't tell you that. I had enough company of my own that I was busy all summer. I'm just getting ready to leave for home myself. After I go to the funeral."

"Did you know Ken Buckley?"

"Everybody knew him. It's terrible, what happened."

"I'm afraid there's been another murder."

"What!" she said, echoing my own reaction.

"Someone in the Kleins' house. It's across the street from where my husband and I are staying in the Margulies's house."

"Can you tell me what happened?"

"Just that a body's been found."

"This is unbelievable. I'm glad I'm leaving. What's going on here?"

"I don't know."

"Is that what you wanted to talk to Dodie Murchison about?"

"I thought she might know the person who I think was murdered."

"She's gone," Jean Hill said. She looked as though she were in a daze. "And Ken Buckley is dead."

"Did you ever see Ken and Dodie together?"

"Did I see them personally? No, I didn't." The implication was clear. "I'm sorry. I really have to sit down and clear my head. This is getting to be a little too much for me."

"I don't know when the homicide took place," Jack said, as I got Eddie's lunch together. "So if Dodie left her place between seven and eight, it doesn't rule her out. If she did it, it would have been earlier. I doubt she would have parked a wagon with her luggage outside the Kleins' house and gone in and murdered someone before walking down to the ferry."

"Do you know who found the body?"

"I don't know anything," he said, sounding exasperated. "I saw Springer race over and zip up the ramp like a maniac and when I got over there, one of the girls who's been living there was sitting on the deck having hysterics."

"I can hardly blame her."

"Marti Jorgensen went over, and some other woman, so she seemed to be in good hands. When I went around the house to find Springer, he shooed me away, along with everybody else. I think he got a bunch of firemen to guard the perimeter."

"I'd like to talk to that girl," I said, picking Eddie up

off the floor and setting him in the high chair. "Ready for lunch?" I asked him.

He gave me a smile and banged on the tray. I took that to be a yes.

"She may still be at the Jorgensens'. Want me to check?" He went to the window that looked out on the Jorgensens' property.

"If you want to," I said.

He waved good-bye to Eddie, who was less interested in his father than his food, and went out the kitchen door. I tried to put together a possible sequence of events. There had been some relationship between Tina and Ken Buckley, although no one I had spoken to had ever seen them together. For some reason, she had gone to see him on Labor Day and murdered him as he lay in bed. (Waiting for her? I wondered.) Dodie had had something going with him herself—that seemed pretty well documented even if Ida Bloom didn't think so—and when she came to the conclusion that Tina had killed Ken, Dodie went over to the Kleins' house and killed Tina. Jealousy? I wondered. But what was there to be jealous about? Ken had had affairs and he had never left his wife before. Why would he do it now?

"It's a mystery," I said to Eddie, who didn't think there was any mystery to lunch. It was just good to eat.

Of course, another voice in my head reminded me, each woman thinks she's the one who'll accomplish the impossible. The "other" woman in a married man's life would always try harder. And Ken had charm, no doubt about that. He had won me over just by being nice to my little Eddie. Chief La Coste obviously revered him, and why not? Ken had visited almost every day. That seemed to me a very kind thing to do for someone who was old and widowed and probably didn't get much farther than the ocean or the bay or a few blocks east or west of his little house.

Eddie plopped his hand into the mushy fruit in front of him and wiped it on his hair. I tried not to laugh. "You are a mess," I said to him.

He said something that sounded like "more."

"Here's some more. But it has to go in your mouth, not in your hair."

He banged his hand on the tray. "You're pretty rambunctious today," I said.

"Ma!"

"I'm Ma. And here's more. Are we learning vowel sounds today?"

He giggled and banged and finally, he drank all his milk. We both looked a mess as Jack came back.

"Looks like a food fight in here. Who won?"

"Who always wins?" I got a washcloth and worked on the little face, against the will of its owner. "Jack, is it OK if I giggle or will he grow up not respecting authority?"

"You have a nice giggle. Almost as nice as Eddie's."

A sweet husband. "Is she there?"

"She's there. Marti's making some lunch for her but I'm not sure she's up to eating it. She'll come over when she's finished."

"Good. We'll get to ours in a few minutes."

13

Her name was Danielle Greene and she looked as though she had suffered a death in the family. Marti brought her over and then left, signalling with her eyes that things were pretty bad.

The three of us sat in the living room, which I had picked up before her arrival so it didn't look as though a baby would crawl out of a corner.

Danielle looked around after she sat down. "I always wondered what it looked like inside," she said, as though she were talking to herself. "I see it every day from the beach and it looks like such a great house."

"We've been enjoying it," I said in a quiet voice.

"You're the one who came over to talk to Tina the night the fire chief died, aren't you?"

I had recognized her, too, as the person who called upstairs to see if Tina would talk to me. "That's right."

She turned to Jack. "And then you came with the policeman the next day and searched the house."

"Right again."

"I don't understand. What do you have to do with all this?"

"I'm a detective sergeant with the NYPD. I offered to help the Blue Harbor police search your house."

"What were you looking for?" She looked confused.

"I saw Tina Frisch near the Buckley house during the fire," I said. "She had a fireman's coat over her back and head and she was pushing her way through the crowd as though she didn't want to be recognized. The police were looking for the coat."

"What was Tina doing at that fire? And why would she have a fireman's coat?"

"That's one of the things I was trying to find out."

"Did you find the coat?"

"It wasn't in your house," Jack said.

"I didn't think it would be."

"Do you know if Tina had any kind of relationship with Ken Buckley? If she knew him at all?"

"I really don't know. She kept to herself a lot. Sometimes she would grab a bike and pedal away. Other times she walked on the beach. I don't know if she was alone or with someone. I spend most of my time out here with my boyfriend."

"I'd like you to tell me everything you know about Tina," I said.

"And if you don't feel comfortable having me around," Jack put in, "I'll go take a walk."

"I don't care. You can stay if you want. I'm probably not too coherent but I'd rather talk to you than the cop."

"Why?" Jack asked quickly.

"He rubs me the wrong way."

"How do you know Tina, Danielle?" I asked.

"We work for the same law firm."

"Have you known her long?"

"A year or so."

"Whose idea was it to rent the house?"

"I don't know. A bunch of us were out for dinner one night after work last winter, and we started talking about what we were going to do in the summer. Maybe it was

Tina's idea. But I'm not sure. All of a sudden, it seemed everyone wanted to rent a house on Fire Island."

"How did you decide on Blue Harbor?"

She thought about that for a minute. "I'm not sure. I guess it was the best house at the best price. I think maybe Tina found the real estate agent. But it could have been someone else."

I didn't ask for the name of the agent. The Kleins would know, if I decided to follow up on that. "Did Tina have a fiancé or boyfriend?"

"No one who ever came out here with her."

"She always came alone?"

"Always."

"Can you tell me who the renters of the house are?"

She went through them, telling me the same thing Jack had reported after Curt Springer had interviewed her on Tuesday. There were three couples, three girls, and three or four guys. One of the guys hadn't come out very often but she was sure he had paid his share. The rental amount for the summer stunned me, but I'm still surprised at what people outside a convent pay for things. I could understand why people who didn't want to use their houses for themselves turned to renters. A summer's income could finance a couple of family vacations, even if there were repairs to be taken care of after the season.

The couples, she explained, were each considered one single, and each actual single was allowed to bring a partner. There were five bedrooms in the Klein house, so there was room for a total of five singles or couples each weekend. They alternated weekends and most of the renters spent their one- or two-week vacations at the house. They would come out on a Sunday night or Monday morning and stay for the next two weeks, including their assigned weekend in the middle, leaving before the Friday crowd

arrived. Danielle and Tina had opted for Labor Day weekend rather than the Fourth of July, and both had decided to
stay until the coming weekend.

"Did Tina ever pair up with any of the single men in
your group?" I asked, when the arrangements seemed
clear.

"I don't think so. She was friendly with everyone, but
I got the feeling she wasn't interested in any of the guys.
I think Kyle was interested in her."

"Kyle? Is that the young man I've seen go by with snorkeling equipment?"

She smiled for the first time, a kind of wistful smile.
"That's Kyle. I don't know what he sees in the water but
it keeps him happy."

"He seems like a very friendly person," I said.

"He is. Warm and fuzzy. I really like him."

"How old is Tina?"

"Twenty-three? Twenty-four?"

"When was the last time you saw Tina, Danielle?"

She swallowed before she answered and I saw her eyes
tear. "It was last night. I saw her a couple of times. She
and Kyle were playing a game in the kitchen when I went
in for a Coke. Then I saw her again later when the woman
came to see her."

"What woman?"

"This young woman, very good-looking, dark hair."

"Tell me about it."

"It was dark already, maybe nine o'clock. She came to
the door and no one was there so she walked in. I was sitting in the living room and I saw her. I asked her what
she wanted and she said she was looking for Tina."

"She mentioned Tina by name?"

"Yes. I don't think she said Frisch. I think she just said
Tina."

"OK."

"So I got up and called Tina and she came down."

"Did Tina know this woman?" I asked.

"It didn't look like it. But I wasn't really listening. I think I heard the woman say her name when Tina came down."

"Do you remember it?"

"No. And maybe that's not what she said. I wasn't really paying attention."

"Then what happened?"

"They went outside."

"For how long?"

"I don't know. My boyfriend came back and we went upstairs."

"Where had your boyfriend been?"

"Swimming. He likes to take a dip in the ocean at night."

"And the two of you went upstairs before Tina came back?"

"We must have. I never saw her again." She began to cry, and I got up and went to the kitchen, feeling very awkward. I poured a couple of glasses of iced tea and carried them back. She murmured a thank-you when she saw it, and she drank it quickly, half of it gone when she put the glass down.

"Did you hear her?"

She shook her head.

"Did you share a bathroom with her?"

She nodded.

"Did you notice if her towel was wet?"

"I didn't notice. And anyway, I think she kept it in her room. There wasn't room in the bathroom for everyone's towels."

"Had you ever seen the dark-haired woman before?"

"I really don't know. Maybe on the beach. You see so many people there. And weekends, when I'm here, there are lots more than during the week."

That was certainly true for most of the summer, although we had come for two of the most crowded weeks, the ones before and after Labor Day. I wasn't sure I would remember someone I passed on the beach, although Jack probably would. He's very observant. "Danielle, who found Tina?"

She pulled a tissue out of her jeans pocket and held it to her face. I heard her whisper in a voice constricted with emotion, "I did."

"I'm so sorry," I said. "It must have been terrible."

"It was. It was the most awful thing that ever happened to me."

"Do you think you can tell us about it?"

She nodded, but it was clear she wasn't ready to talk yet. She drank the rest of her tea and Jack got up and took the glass to the kitchen. I waited without saying anything. Jack had returned with a fresh glass before she was able to speak.

"I went outside." Her face was wet with tears, her voice barely audible. "I needed the bike. I was going to the store at the bay." She paused a minute. "The bike is around the side of the house, near the back. We keep it behind the latticework. There's a kind of gate there. They told us to keep it closed because the deer can get in."

Deer were a problem on Fire Island. They wandered off the grounds of the parks, leaving ticks in the grasses and getting their antlers tangled in the crawl spaces under the houses on stilts. I had heard it was a messy business trying to get them out.

"I understand," I said.

"I pulled the gate open and—" She was crying again.

"She was in there. Tina. I touched her and I screamed. I ran into the house and someone called the police."

I knew, of course, exactly when the phone call had come. I was just leaving Curt Springer's office when he answered the phone and dashed out. I remembered what he had said: "Don't touch anything." He had been thinking of the crime scene.

"Was the bicycle in there?" I asked.

"I think so. I think she was lying on top of it."

"Was there any blood?"

"I'm not sure. I don't remember seeing any."

We still didn't know how she had been murdered. "Did you notice what she was wearing?"

"I think—I think it could have been what she was wearing last night."

"So she could have been murdered last night and her body might have been hidden for ten or twelve hours."

"It's possible."

I was about to ask about the other members of the household when a man's voice called from the kitchen, "Anyone home?"

Jack went to see who it was and came back with the young man I often saw walk by with snorkeling gear.

"Hi, I'm Kyle Holbrook. How's it going, Danny?"

"Not so great."

We introduced ourselves and invited him to sit down, and Jack got another glass of iced tea. Kyle's feet were bare. I had never seen such a huge pair of feet.

"Were you home last night?" I asked him.

"All night. Tina and I played a couple of games and then I read for a while."

"Were you there when Tina had a visitor?"

"The good-looking gal, yeah. Dodie something."

"You heard her name?"

"Just the Dodie part. Tina came down and they went outside."

"Did you hear anything they said?"

"They must have waited till they were outside to talk. I heard their voices for a coupla minutes but that was all. They must've walked away."

"Did you hear them again? When they came back?"

"No. I went in the kitchen for a beer and then I went upstairs."

"Do you remember when?"

"Maybe ten. Maybe later."

"Did you see Tina again?"

"Nope."

"Did you hear her when you were upstairs?"

"I can't tell who I hear when I'm upstairs."

"So you never saw her after she walked out of the house with Dodie?"

"Never."

"Anyone else come into the house last night?" Jack asked.

"Just the guys who live there."

"Do you lock the door at night?" I asked.

Kyle and Danielle exchanged looks. "We fight about that," he said. "Some guys want to lock it, some don't give a . . . damn," he said, making a quick try at cleaning up his language, probably on my behalf. "It's a pain to carry a key."

"So it wasn't locked?"

"Probably not."

"Did you know this Dodie woman? Had you seen her or talked to her?"

"I saw her on the beach. I think I ran into her once in the liquor store. I never met her."

"Did Tina ever mention her to either of you?"

They looked at each other, but both said no.

"You'd never seen her at your house before?"

Their nos were stronger this time.

"How long are you both staying in Blue Harbor?" I asked.

"I want to get out of here as soon as I can," Danielle said. "And I never want to come back. We're supposed to be out by tomorrow anyway. The Kleins let us stay on this week after Labor Day but I think they're coming out tomorrow to assess the damage." She said this disparagingly, as though the Kleins assumed the renters had torn apart their house when, in fact, they had cared for it well. "Will we still have to talk to that cop?"

"You will," Jack said. "He's going to have to get a statement from everyone in the house. He's probably looking for you now. He may not be happy that we've spoken to you before he could get to you. I would guess he's been busy with the county people and he's probably talked to whoever's in the house."

"That's what he was doing when I left," Kyle said. "He's asking everyone about the earring."

Jack and I spoke at almost the same moment. "What earring?"

"Didn't you hear? One of Tina's diamond earrings is missing. I never saw her without it."

"Nor I," I said. I glanced at Danielle, who looked confused. "Was it—was it ripped off her ear?"

"Nah." Kyle spoke almost casually. "Looked like someone had removed it without pulling it off. You know, like unscrewed it. They're in two parts, aren't they?" He looked at Danielle, who nodded. "Those crime scene guys are combing the grass for it. You think that Dodie killed Tina?" he asked us.

"I wouldn't hazard a guess," Jack said. "I'd like to

know what Chief Springer found, how Tina was killed, how long she's been dead. Is there any other house she could have spent the night in?"

They didn't seem to think so, especially, Danielle said, because she hadn't made many friends. She had kept to herself, hadn't gone out at night, hadn't seemed interested in socializing.

Of course there was Chief La Coste, I thought. And it was possible that I was the only one who knew about that.

Jack walked Danielle back to the house, but Kyle stayed behind.

"She found Tina, you know," he said.

"She told us. It must have been the worst moment of her life." I had found some bodies myself in the last couple of years, since I almost inadvertently started investigating murders, and I knew how terrible it was, even the time when I expected to find one. In Danielle's case, it was a surprise and a shock, and to make matters worse, it was the body of a friend. "Is there anything you can tell me about Tina that might help in finding her killer? I have a special reason for being interested. I saw her come out of the Buckley house during the fire and although I spoke to her, she denied she'd been there and denied we had spoken."

"She was a strange person," Kyle said. "I liked her. I was interested in her, but she didn't seem interested in anything this summer."

"Maybe she was recovering from a relationship that ended," I suggested.

"Could be. She didn't talk much about herself, just her job and how she and Danny had decided to come out here. She kept to herself, took a lot of long walks. She didn't sit out on the beach, said she burned easily, but she went in the water once in a while, usually early in the day or after the sun was at its hottest."

"Makes sense if you burn. Were you involved in selecting the house?"

"Nah. I didn't do anything except write a check. Some of the others came out in the spring to look at it but I didn't bother. I heard it was close to the beach so I said, count me in."

"Did she tell you why she came to Fire Island?"

"She said she'd always wanted to come here, said she'd heard a lot about it."

"Did she ever mention Ken Buckley, the fire chief who died in the fire on Monday?"

"Not to me."

"Where were you during that fire?"

"I was on the beach. I saw the smoke and I saw everyone running but I stayed where I was."

"Did you see Tina?"

"I saw her before the fire. We were walking on the beach together."

"And then what?" I said.

"She said she had somewhere to go."

"And she left you?"

"Yeah."

"You're sure she left the beach before the fire?"

"Oh, yeah. Half an hour or so. She went up the dune, back toward the house."

I wasn't surprised that Tina had lied to me about walking on the beach during the fire. I knew where she'd been, but this was corroborating evidence that her walk had ended before the fire.

"This Dodie woman," I said. "Did you happen to see her around the time of the fire?"

"I don't remember. I could've. She's a gorgeous woman. I liked to look at her. I was surprised when she came to the house last night. I wondered what connection she could have to Tina."

"I wish I knew," I said.

14

Jack came back just as Kyle was leaving. "I've got the Kleins' phone number," he said. "I think we should call them. Springer's looking for a killer in one direction, but I think the way we're going will be more fruitful."

I agreed. I told him what Kyle had said, and added, "It sounds like Tina had somewhere to go before the Buckley fire."

"The question is, did she shoot Ken? And if she did, what's the connection between her and Dodie?"

"I may be the connection. I told Dodie I'd seen Tina outside the Buckley house on Labor Day. Dodie asked me for Tina's name and where she lived. She may have wanted to ask Tina what her interest in Ken Buckley was. But I find it hard to believe she killed her."

"So do I. For a lot of reasons. Springer told me Tina's neck was broken. That's not an easy thing to do. Of course, nowadays New York women take courses in self-protection, and maybe Dodie's went one step further."

I smiled but said nothing.

"Another thing is, she's a young professional with her whole career ahead of her. She walked into that house last night and people saw her. She said her name aloud and people heard it. Killers don't announce their arrival and ask if the victim is available. I mean, not if they have a brain in their head."

"Maybe she just wanted to check out for herself what I told her, that Tina was around the Buckley house and then denied it."

"So what did she find out from Tina that made her leave early this morning?"

"As usual, the question I can't answer. She's probably home by now. We'll have to try to call her there."

"Give Springer a crack at her first. She's a suspect in a homicide, even if she's an unlikely one. I'm going to give the Kleins a call and find out who their realtor is. And we gotta think about that missing earring."

I was glad he'd volunteered to make the call. I'd never make a very good telemarketer; I hate calling strangers, and you have to do that a lot when you look into a homicide.

He came back with notes. "Here's the Kleins' phone number. Here's their realtor, Bea Rice. I talked to her, but she's not the one who actually showed the house to the renters. She was the listing agent. The one the groupers called was this one, Honey Quinn."

"Honey as in honey pot?"

"Sounds like it. You want to give her a ring?"

"Why not?" I took the notes and went to the kitchen.

The voice that answered, "Island Homes, Honey Quinn speaking," was deep with tobacco and perhaps something stronger.

"Ms. Quinn, my name is Chris Bennett and I'm spending a couple of weeks at a friend's house in Blue Harbor."

"Whose house, may I ask?"

"Max Margulies."

"Oh. That's a *great* house. You must be loving it."

"We are. Ms. Quinn—"

"Honey, Chris. I'm Honey to everybody."

I was "honey" only to my husband and it made me feel a little uncomfortable, but business is business. "Honey, I have some questions about the Klein house. It's just across the street and down the—"

"I know where it is." I could hear her exhale what was probably smoke. "What's your question?"

"Do you remember which of those people called you looking for a place to rent for the summer?"

"Sure, I remember. Tina Frisch. Nice gal. Said it had to be Blue Harbor and big was better than small. Some reason you're asking?"

"I'll explain in a minute. I just wanted to know if she had any other requirements, you know, that it should be near this or that or any particular family."

"Well, they'd all like to be on the water but that's impossible most of the time."

"How many houses did she look at?"

"Let's see. She came out one weekend—I'd have to check my files to remind myself when—and looked at about five houses. She put a deposit down before she left."

"Do you know why she picked this one?"

"It was the best house she looked at. The others were smaller or didn't have as many bathrooms. The usual complaints."

"How long did she want to rent for?"

"Hold on." Small noises indicated a quick search. Smoke. "The Kleins wanted to rent from water on to water off—"

"What?"

"From last frost to first frost, you know, when you turn on the water in the spring and when you turn it off in the fall, but the group didn't want it that long and they didn't want to pay that much. So they negotiated it down to Memorial Day weekend to Labor Day and then they dickered and got this extra week. Till Friday. That's tomorrow."

"Do you remember her asking anything at all about the people who lived in Blue Harbor?"

More smoke. "Yeah. She asked the names of the neighbors."

"Do you know why?"

"I think she wanted to see if she knew any of them."

"Did she?"

"Sounded like she didn't. So why all the questions?"

"Tina died, Honey."

"What?"

"I think it happened last night. The police are investigating it right now. I got to know her a little, and some of the things she said made me curious."

"Do the Kleins know?"

"I believe they've been informed. I'm asking you these questions because there seem to be strange circumstances associated with her death." I tried to be as oblique as possible. I didn't want to use the word murder.

"My God. This has never happened to me before."

I didn't bother mentioning that it hadn't happened to Tina either, and what had happened to her was more serious and more permanent. "If there's anything you can remember about Tina or the rental transaction, I'd be interested to know."

"There was something," the voice grated out. "I told you she asked about the neighbors? Well, when I gave her the names, she said something a little weird. She seemed pleased that she didn't know any of them."

"That's interesting."

"Something about wanting to keep to herself, being private. You know what I mean?"

"I think so."

"In fact—you know, it's coming back to me. I think I remember what she said. It was something like, 'Good. They're all strangers.' "

*   *   *

"Sounds like we're getting somewhere," Jack said, after I'd told him what Honey Quinn said. "Finally. I was starting to think we had a million pieces that all fitted into different puzzles."

I had had a similar feeling myself. "Tina had a reason for spending weekends in Blue Harbor. Somehow Ken Buckley was part of that reason. I keep remembering that hug that Eve gave her when they talked yesterday morning. Could they have been in something together?" I wasn't really asking Jack for answers; I was thinking of questions that had to be answered, and we were both making notes in our idiosyncratic ways, Jack with his folded sheets of paper, I in my steno-type notebook.

"We talked about this before," I said, "that Eve and Tina could have murdered Ken together. But who is Tina to Ken Buckley?"

"Or to Eve."

"Or to Eve, yes. And it would be pretty hard to prove that Eve killed Tina. There have to be dozens of witnesses who'll place her at Ken's wake. And the last ferry is about when Dodie dropped in to see Tina last night."

"So we could be dealing with two killers."

I considered this. "Tina kills Ken and someone kills Tina for killing Ken."

"At least that theory gives a motive for the second murder."

"I suppose one motive is better than none." I looked at my watch. Eddie would be getting up soon and I really wanted a swim in the freshwater pool. Getting to the bottom of a homicide was satisfying, but swimming in freshwater on a hot afternoon was a taste of heaven. "Jack, we need to talk to Dodie. Even if Springer has to talk to her first, she's the only person who knows why she went to see Tina last night. I bet the Goodwins have her home number."

"Sounds reasonable."

"I'm going to call Jean Hill, the next-door neighbor, and see if she'll give it to me."

She gave it readily, having heard through the Blue Harbor grapevine about Tina's murder. The Goodwins, she assured me, already knew about it. I didn't have to ask who had told them.

Mrs. Goodwin was talkative and inquisitive, and a short phone call stretched into a longer one, but I came away with Dodie's phone number. Eddie had begun making sounds while Mrs. Goodwin was talking, and Jack had gone upstairs. I dialed Dodie's number—it was a Manhattan one—and let it ring. An answering machine picked up and a man's voice invited me to leave a message. I declined.

The three of us went to the pool and had a refreshing swim. It was almost empty, with no one there of school age, which made it easy to swim laps without running into a child. I could see there were advantages to visiting a resort when school was in session.

When I'd swum enough to make me feel ready to conquer the world, I took Eddie and let Jack have his chance. Jack is one of those natural strong swimmers who does two laps for every one that I do and he's really a pleasure to watch as he cuts through the water, but I gave Eddie all my attention as he tried to propel himself with hands and legs moving furiously and no coordination at all. What was clear to me was that he loved the water as much as I did, and I knew my future held many summers at the Oakwood pool.

* * *

We had to walk past the Kleins' house to get to ours. It was now about six hours since Tina's body had been discovered. A crime scene investigation generally takes at least that and often much longer. In this case, the county people first had to come out to the island. I could see they had cordoned off the whole area along the side and back of the house. The yellow plastic tape read POLICE—CRIME SCENE endlessly, like the tape around the Buckley house. Danielle saw us and waved, turning her hand into a thumbs-down. I guessed she'd had to rehash her terrible story for Curt Springer.

Springer himself walked down the ramp just at that moment and called to Jack to wait. "Well, how are you folks?"

We said something innocuous and he went on. "Sorry I tore out of there this morning, Mrs. Brooks. All I heard on the phone was that there was a body."

"I understand."

"I guess you know Miss Murchison came to see Miss Frisch last night."

"We heard," Jack said. "Have you talked to her yet?"

"She doesn't answer her phone and the neighbors haven't seen her. Not that New Yorkers ever notice what their neighbors are doing anyway. I called her precinct in Manhattan to check it out." He seemed impressed that he was dealing with a New York City precinct. "We've got the crime scene guys over at her Blue Harbor house right now picking up latents. There are plenty of prints on the gate back here and on the bike. I want to see if anything matches up with the prints in the house she's been living in."

"You figure her for a suspect?" Jack asked.

"She's the last person who saw Tina Frisch alive. I'm coming around to consider her a suspect. What do you think?"

"Unless you find someone who saw her later, I'd say Murchison's a possible. Any idea when the victim died?"

"Last night is the best anyone'll say right now. They'll do an autopsy tomorrow and then we'll know for sure."

"So it's possible the body wasn't found for nine or ten hours."

"That's what they're telling me." He looked at his watch. "The neighbor next door to Murchison saw her pulling a wagon to the ferry about seven this morning. You'd think she could get back to Manhattan in eight hours."

"Maybe she had plans for the weekend," I suggested.

"You never can tell, but if we don't locate her pretty soon, I'll have to put out an alarm for her car."

I didn't say it, but I had to agree that even six hours was more than twice as long as she needed to get from the ferry to Manhattan, especially after rush hour.

"What's the story on the missing earring?" Jack asked.

"That's something, isn't it? One earring gone. They went over the whole area with a metal detector. No sign of it. Find that earring, you'll find her killer."

"Will you keep me posted on the prints, Curt?"

"Sure will. The crime scene boys'll be taking all that with them when they leave tonight. Shouldn't take too long to find a match."

"Anything more on the Buckley homicide?"

"Well, I've got to believe this is related, don't you think?"

"Looks that way," Jack said.

"And I guess I owe you an apology, Mrs. Brooks. When you told me that Tina Frisch was at the Buckley fire with a fireman's coat over her, I thought you might be on to something until I talked to Miss Frisch. She was adamant she hadn't been there, hadn't seen you, never saw a fireman's coat in her life. Now it seems you may have been right."

"Well," I said, trying to be generous, "when you hear conflicting stories, you can't believe them both."

"Sorry I picked the wrong one in this case. What do you suppose she did with that coat?"

I had no desire to bring Chief La Coste into this mess, so I said I didn't know. For all I knew, the chief had his own coat, as he had his own somewhat out-of-date uniform. Had he lent it to Tina? I couldn't say. Had she taken a coat from somewhere else and dropped it off at his house? Impossible to answer.

We thanked Springer and walked home.

15

We played with Eddie on the living room floor until it was time for his bath and dinner. He babbled almost without stopping, as though he had something very important to tell us and we just weren't getting it. He looked very intense, his face a small, very young version of his father's. It gave me warm feelings to see how one generation inherited what was most important from the preceding one.

When we were able to talk, I said to Jack, "What would you think of my calling Sister Joseph and inviting her out for tomorrow and the day after?"

"Interesting idea. You thinking of her well-being or you want to see what she makes of this case?"

"Both. I know it's a long drive from St. Stephen's, but I bet she's never been here and I think seeing a magnificent sunset is almost a religious experience."

"You making up her excuses?"

"She's clever enough to make up her own, and besides, she doesn't need any. And the truth is, at this point what we know doesn't make much sense, and except for interviewing Dodie, I don't know where to look for new information."

"Springer's prints may give us some."

"It won't be conclusive, whichever way it goes. If Dodie's prints aren't anywhere around the Klein house, what does it tell us? That she didn't touch anything there.

We know she was there. That's been confirmed by two witnesses. And suppose her prints are there. She could have helped Tina pull the bike out of the crawl space. It doesn't mean she put Tina's body inside."

"So Murchison opens the gate and then says toodle-ooh?"

"Why not? They're talking about something, Tina says she wants to take a ride somewhere. they walk back to the crawl space and say good-bye."

"You should be a defense attorney."

I smiled. "I have a busy schedule right now. I'll leave that to you."

"You're right that it won't be conclusive, but every little bit of evidence placing Murchison at the crime scene is bad for her."

"Which she knows, Jack. She may specialize in writing wills and organizing estates but she knows the law. If she kills Tina and stuffs her body in the crawl space, she knows eventually someone will match her prints with the ones she's leaving behind."

"So there won't be any to find."

"So it means nothing. How do you feel about my giving Sister Joseph a ring?"

"Go to it. We've got an extra bedroom. She can have as much privacy as she wants, and if I remember correctly, she eats anything."

"You remember right. Keep an eye on Eddie and I'll make the call. I think I can catch her before evening prayers."

"You're not going to tell me you've stumbled on a body on Fire Island," Joseph said, when she picked up the phone.

"Two bodies. How are you?"

We exchanged enough conversation to bring each other

up to date on health and family. Then Joseph said, "Does that mean I can expect a visit?"

"Actually, no. It means I'm inviting you to come here tomorrow and stay over one night at least." I thought I'd give her the option of longer or shorter. There was a Catholic church in a nearby town if she wanted to try it. "We have a comfortable extra bedroom with two beds and you're welcome to bring one of the nuns along."

"This is very tempting."

"I'm glad. You can leave St. Stephen's whatever time you want tomorrow, the earlier the better, and call me from the ferry. I'll be there with a wagon to carry your luggage."

"A wagon for my luggage! Chris, how much luggage do I need for an overnight stay?"

"As much as you want to take. Will you come?"

"I will be delighted."

I had offered an invitation to a second nun in case she felt more comfortable not traveling and staying overnight alone. In the old days, sisters were not allowed to visit anyone in their homes. Visits were generally made only to family members, and the nun would spend the night in a nearby convent. During the years that I had visited my aunt on a regular basis, I had done so with the permission of the Superior. My aunt was family and also widowed, so she lived alone, and I had stayed with her in a room she considered mine.

Also, in times gone by, nuns traveled in pairs. Things are very different today but I wanted Joseph to have the option of doing what made her most comfortable. I would reimburse her for her travel expenses, as her allowance was very small, and I wouldn't dream of asking her to pay for this trip.

I was thrilled she was coming. I told Eddie all about

her as I bathed him. He had met her a couple of times, but not for a few months. As I soaped him up and rinsed him off, I tried to get him to say "Joseph" or at least "Joe." He looked at me as though I were nuts and I got nowhere. But we would have time to work on it the next morning.

Jack and I went outside after dinner, talking about what we would cook for Joseph, what we should show her, how we would cover the mirror in the upstairs bathroom, as Aunt Meg had covered the one in the house we now own and live in for all those years I visited once a month as a nun. We sat on the deck in the cool sea breeze and I felt very lucky that Melanie hadn't been able to use her uncle's house, that this enormous luxury had dropped in our laps.

It was cool this evening, cooler than it had been since our arrival, a sign of the fall to come, and there were few people below us on the beach. A couple of hours ago Tina's body had been wheeled on a gurney to the bay, where it had been placed on a boat belonging to the sheriff's department. Marti had come by earlier to tell us.

We had brought out a tray of coffee and cake and a glass of brandy for Jack, who was enjoying the last days of his first vacation in a long time. Monday he would head back to the Sixty-fifth Precinct in Brooklyn and resume his job as detective sergeant. And next week I also would return to my job of teaching poetry at a local college not too far from where we lived. In other words, summer would be more than officially over; it would be over in fact. I didn't look forward to leaving Fire Island. I had never had a vacation as sumptuous and restful as this one, or as inexpensive. I was happy that Jack had been able to spend all these days with his son, to indulge himself. When he returned to work next week he would also return to law school four nights of the week. There would be no more lazy meals, late-night brandies, afternoon naps, reading for pleasure.

"I tried Dodie's number again," I said, as Jack poured the coffee. "No answer."

"She went somewhere else. Or she's not answering the phone. Looks funny either way. I'd guess Springer'll have her car in the alarms in the morning."

"You think Tina killed Ken Buckley?"

"I don't know what to think. Where's the gun?"

"She could have taken the ferry back to the mainland and tossed it during the trip. Then came back without it."

"That's a possibility. I think we'd've found it if she had it in the house."

"Did you look in the crawl space?"

He thought about it. "I didn't," he said. "Maybe Springer did."

I looked out over the beach. A dark figure with a lighted cigarette was moving towards us. "We may be getting interesting company," I said.

The figure came closer. "Evening, folks," a familiar voice called.

"Good evening, Chief." I stood and went to greet him. "Will you join us for coffee?"

"Gave up coffee a long time ago."

"Maybe brandy," Jack said, rising. "I'm Chris's husband, Jack Brooks."

"Nice to meet you. You've got a lovely wife and a real cute little baby. Now I see who he takes after. What was that you were offering?"

"I've got a bottle of brandy here and some pretty good cake."

"They both sound good." He settled into one of the chairs. "Nice cool evening. Feels a little like autumn. Guess I've managed to clock another summer."

"You've got a lot more, Chief," I said. "You just took a long walk to get here."

"I like to walk at night. The beach is empty. It's quiet. If you haven't seen the moon over the ocean, you haven't lived."

Jack came back with the bottle, a glass, and another plate and fork. He poured the brandy and the chief took a sip and closed his eyes.

"Reminds me of good times," he said. "These are very bad times right now."

"They are," I agreed. "The murder was just down the street from here."

"That was a nice young lady, a nice girl, if you'll permit me to use an old-fashioned word."

"She seemed very nice."

"A quarter of my age and she's gone. If I felt terrible when Ken died, how can I even explain how I feel now? Little more than a child and this happens to her."

"Did you know her, sir?" Jack asked.

"I knew her. Not too well, but I knew her." He put his glass down on the little table next to him and looked straight at me. "I lied to you, Chris," he said. "I told you I didn't know Tina, but I did. Knew her since July."

I felt a tingle in my arms that was not from the cold night air. He had come to tell me what I had been trying to get out of him since Tuesday. "Will you tell me about it?" I asked.

"I'll tell you now that it's too late. I'll tell you what I know but it ain't much. She came to me one day in July, can't tell you exactly when, a weekend probably. That's when you see the groupers mostly. Said she was renting a big house with a group of young people but she wasn't here for the sunshine and the beach. She was here because someone in her family disappeared a long time ago and

the last time anyone knew where he was, he was supposed to be going out to Fire Island."

"There are a lot of places on Fire Island he could have
come to."

"That's just what I said to her, but she was sure it was
Blue Harbor. Said her mother or someone in the family
had heard him say where he was going. And he never
came back."

"Or if he did," Jack said, "he didn't let his family
know."

"That's what I told her. We think the same way, you
and me. Just because someone comes out here, doesn't
mean he didn't go back on the ferry and then disappear."

"When did this happen?"

"Well, she's about twenty-three, twenty-four now. She
was a little girl of eight when 'Uncle Bill' got lost. That's
what she called him. Uncle Bill. Last name, 'James,' or
something like that. So that would make it—what? Fifteen years ago? That's a long time ago to be trying to find
someone."

"Did she say what he was coming out here for? Was he
visiting someone?"

"I got the feeling there was a girlfriend with him."

"I don't suppose she told you who that was."

"I don't know if she knew," the old man said. "The
first thing the family thought was that he'd drowned. It
happens. It's happened here. Not this year, not last year,
but we've had our troubles. She thought maybe he swam
out too far or went swimming at night and got swept
away."

"Did he know how to swim?"

"She said he was a good swimmer. Bein' a good
swimmer never stopped anybody from drowning."

I told him I agreed with him. It was the people I knew
who were good swimmers who sometimes took chances

because of their belief in their own ability to cope with high waves and possible undertows. The less able were often less secure and took fewer chances. "Were there any bodies washed ashore fifteen years ago?"

"Not in my memory and not in the police files. Course, not every body washes ashore."

"Did she check with Chief Springer?"

"It was before his time. I checked the files, what there was of them. Nothing that year, nothing the year before, nothing the year after. So," he said, anticipating my next question, "I called up my old buddy Jerry O'Donnell, the last police chief before young Curt. He didn't remember anything about a drowning or a body swept ashore or anybody missing in his last coupla years as chief. One big, fat dead end."

"Did she look into anything else? A fight, maybe?"

"Well, I went through those police records myself and I couldn't find anything. There are always fights, especially in summer, young fellas boozin' it up, don't know when to stop. I couldn't find a Bill or a William who got himself in trouble those years. So what do you think?"

I knew what I thought. I just wasn't sure whether I should say it. "I think she started thinking about fires and she went to see Ken Buckley."

"Now that's good thinkin'," the chief said. "Because she asked me about fires. There was that big one I told you about, but no one was hurt in that one. There were a few smaller ones, but no one got hurt in those either. So who knows?"

"Did she talk to Ken?" I asked.

"I can't say for a fact that she did. She asked me who the chief was and where the firehouse was and where he lived. But she never came out and said she'd talked to him."

"There's some speculation she killed Ken," I said.

"Well, that's just dumb. She had a gun and she went over and shot him? And then what? Set the house on fire? You really think somethin' like that happened?"

"It's what people are saying," Jack said. "Chris and I think there's more to it. Is there anything else you know that could help us?"

"She thought she was getting close," the chief said, looking beyond both of us. "But that's all I know."

"Chief, I did see Tina at the Buckley house fire. And she saw me, although she denied it later. She had a fireman's coat over her back and head. Jack and Curt Springer searched the house she was living in and the jacket wasn't there. Did she leave it at your house?"

I sensed he didn't want to answer that, but I thought he would. He had come here to tell us what he knew. Finally he said, "Yeah. She gave it to me to hold for her."

"When?"

"Must've been Monday night. Labor Day."

So it was already gone when Curt Springer and Jack went through the house. "Is it your coat, Chief?"

"No sir, not mine. Never saw it before."

"Don't they have names in them? So the firemen take the right one?"

"We do that ourselves here in Blue Harbor, write our names somewhere in that indelible black ink. This one— well, someone had inked over the name good and heavy. I couldn't tell you whose it was. But it wasn't mine, I promise you that."

"Maybe she grabbed it off the truck," Jack said.

"Truck wasn't nowheres near the house. It was on the beach. They run the hose from the pumper truck but that truck's too wide to go through any street except Main Street. You didn't see a truck there, did you?"

"Now that I think of it, I didn't."

"So Tina went to the Buckley house with someone's

jacket, or she found one at the Buckleys' and grabbed it. When she got home, she inked out the name inside because she knew I'd seen her and she'd have to get rid of it."

"That's good thinkin'," the chief said. "Glad to see young folks with a brain. You hear some a that stuff they call music nowadays, you wonder if they got anything up there."

"It's funny," I said, more to Jack than to the chief. "If you have a gun, you can toss it overboard from a boat, but if you have a thick coat stuffed with puffy, heat-resistant material, it's not easy to get rid of it in the water. And you can't dig a hole in Blue Harbor to bury it without hitting water pretty quick."

"Makes it hard to get rid of a body, too," the chief said, "just in case you were thinking of burying one."

"That should keep the murder rate down on this island, but right now it isn't working. Do you still have the coat?"

"I got it."

"I think you ought to give it to Chief Springer. It may be evidence in a homicide."

"I guess you're right. But it won't bring that poor little girl back, will it?"

Jack insisted on walking the chief home, and, after his brandy was topped off, the chief relented. I cleared the dishes and went inside as the men started off along the dark beach.

16

"That was a crock of bull," Jack said, with more vehemence than he usually expressed. He had walked in the front door from the beach while I was picking up the living room in anticipation of tomorrow's guest.

"You think he was lying?"

"I think Tina's story about 'Uncle Bill' was a fairy tale. She was looking for something all right, but it wasn't 'Uncle Bill.' "

"It didn't even have to be a man," I said. "If a body had been washed up on the beach at the right time, she would have known it was the person she was looking for. But there's no record of a drowning."

"Or a fight, or a fatal fire. Maybe her father was cheating on her mother and he came out here and was never seen again."

"Maybe it was her mother. We don't know anything about her family."

"Whatever else she lied about, I have to believe the time element was true. She wouldn't say something happened fifteen years ago if it happened five years ago. So we have to start with that. What was Ken Buckley doing fifteen years ago, and how is he tied into this?"

"He wasn't fire chief then, I'm sure of that. But he was a fireman."

"And he was here in Blue Harbor so he was a better

source of information for Tina than Springer. And the older firemen, like the two guys we talked to yesterday afternoon. We don't have much time, Chris. This is Thursday night."

"I haven't wanted to think about that. These two weeks have just flown."

"Well, Eddie's become a swimmer. That's something."

"It is something. Jack, do you suppose they have records of old fires at the firehouse?"

"They have to be somewhere, either there or at the municipal building next door. What time is Sister Joseph coming?"

"When she gets here. She'll call before she gets on the ferry."

"That'll give us half an hour's warning. But one of us'll have to stay home."

I smiled. "We'll flip a coin in the morning."

"Sounds like equal opportunity to me."

I'm not sure who won the toss, but at nine the next morning I dashed over to the firehouse. Firemen of all ages and their wives were assembling in preparation for a march to the ferry. The man named Fred had settled into a card game with another man I hadn't met.

"Chris Brooks, right?" Fred said, as I walked over.

"You have a good memory. I need some help I'm sure you can give me." I felt embarrassed flattering him so openly, but he gave me a big smile.

"At your service." He put his cards down on the table and got up, introduced me to Mike, who put his cards down, too, and rose just far enough to shake my hand. Both men were wearing black ties and black armbands.

"Have there been any fatal fires in Blue Harbor as long as you've been here?"

"Never had one in the history of the town," Mike called from the table, where he had lit a cigar.

"Any fires where people required hospitalization?"

Fred said there hadn't been. Once someone had burned a hand badly enough to require medical attention, but that was the worst he could remember.

"Are there records of the fires you've been called out on?"

"In the chief's office. Very good records. Want to see them? They're open to the public. We've got nothing to hide."

We went into a small office, and I remembered that when we first came to the firehouse with Eddie and met Buckley, he had walked out of that room. There were file cabinets, a desk, a telephone, and some shelves built into the wall that displayed models of old fire engines and little lead firemen in uniforms from long ago.

On the walls were photographs of Ken Buckley with various well-known people, including former Governor Cuomo of New York and former Mayor Koch of New York City. Arranged along one wall were framed pictures of former fire chiefs in Blue Harbor, including a couple of pictures of Chief La Coste. There were also pictures dating back to before the Second World War of the Blue Harbor Fire Department members standing in front of their trucks.

"Like a museum, isn't it?" Fred said.

"I'm very impressed. You must be a great bunch of people. Do the models belong to the fire department or to Ken Buckley?"

"A little of both. He said he'd leave them all to us in his will. But who knows if he got to put it in? A man doesn't expect to die at such a young age."

I agreed with him and asked him to show me the records of past fires. There weren't many, even small ones.

If the fire department had disappeared for weeks on end, no one would have noticed. I found the fire where the man needed medical attention for his hand. That was the only fire that year.

I went back in time, glancing at the records. It took no time to reach the Great Fire of Blue Harbor. At that point, I took out my notebook and wrote down everything that seemed relevant, including the names of the home-owners, the addresses, the descriptions of the damage.

"Were you involved in the big fire fifteen years ago?" I asked Fred.

"Oh, yeah. Never forget that. It was the end of the summer. We got the call and we ran. By the time we got there, I could see there wasn't much we could save. It was a one-story frame and it was a real worker. We hadda wet down the houses on either side to make sure the fire didn't spread. I been a summer fireman for twenty-five years and nothing ever came close to that in my experience."

"Was anyone hurt?"

"Thank God, everyone got outta there safe and sound." He rapped his knuckles on the wooden desk.

"What happened to the people who lived there?"

"Oh, they moved."

"Where?"

He frowned. "I don't remember, but west of here, one of the bigger towns. You'll find them in the book. But they can't tell you nothin'. They weren't there."

"If they weren't there, how did the fire start?"

He shrugged. "Read what it says. That file's got all your answers."

"You must have had help from the towns east and west of here."

"We did. A fire like that, one company can't handle it. Like with the Buckley house. All the towns around here, we have mutual-aid agreements with all the other towns. We get a big one, we call a multiple alarm and the other companies respond. And we go if they call. You can't ever have too many firefighters at the scene of a real working fire."

"Was Chief La Coste at that fire?"

"Bernie? You know how old he was fifteen years ago? Seventy-seven. He's been inactive longer'n I've been here."

"But I bet he came to see it."

"Bernie wouldn't miss a fire. But I was too busy fighting that fire to see who was there."

"I suppose there was a big insurance claim."

"You got me. I don't know anything about that."

"Was Ken at that fire?"

"I would guess so."

"Fred?" a woman's voice called.

"Hey, sorry. That's my wife. We must be going down to the ferry now. I gotta close up the office."

"Thanks very much, Fred." I walked out of the office, and he locked the door as he closed it.

There was a large group now, and the men had put their ties on and were all wearing black armbands. They were as somber a group as I had ever seen. I ducked out of the firehouse as they were assembling into a marching group.

At home, Jack assured me there had been no phone calls.

"I have one to make," I said. "I have to think who can help me. Mel's probably back at school by now. I'll have to call Arnold. He always knows the answer to everything."

Arnold Gold, attorney-at-law, had become a surrogate father to me since I met him during my first murder investigation three years ago this summer. He is also my occasional part-time employer and as good a friend as I have ever had. I dialed his number at work in downtown Manhattan and a familiar voice answered. When I gave her my name, she switched me to Arnold.

"Haven't heard your happy voice for a while. How's my surrogate grandson?"

"Thriving. Arnold, I have to keep this line free because I'm expecting a phone call. I need a quick piece of information."

"You're not going to tell me you're looking for a killer on your vacation?"

"Possibly a double killer, possibly two killers."

"On Fire Island? New York's great vacation spot?"

"Afraid so. Do you have an almanac handy? Or some reference book that'll tell me what day of the week a fifteen-year-old date was?"

"I do indeed, if I can just put my hands on it. What's your date?"

I gave it to him.

"Early September. Ah. Here it is. Just a second. I'm going to put the phone down."

I waited impatiently, wanting both to get off the phone and to find out what he would tell me. I didn't want Joseph to miss her chance to call from the other side of the bay.

"Here it is. It's a Monday. The first Monday in September."

"So that would be Labor Day."

"Every year I can remember. Does that make you happy?"

"Happy isn't the word for it. I'll call you when I have a minute. I can't thank you enough."

"You owe me a story, Chrissie."

"You'll get it. Love to Harriet." I hung up.

What were the chances of the two biggest fires in Blue Harbor taking place on Labor Day? Not very great, I thought, unless they were connected.

17

Five minutes later the phone rang, and Joseph said she would hop on the next ferry, which was scheduled to leave in about seven minutes. That gave me thirty-seven minutes to think about what I had just learned.

"You on the phone with Arnold?" Jack asked, coming into the kitchen where Eddie was crawling around and tossing small toys.

"He checked a date for me. You know that fire that Chief La Coste calls 'the Great Fire'? It happened on Labor Day."

"Very nice." Jack opened the refrigerator. Eddie crawled over and grabbed Jack's leg. "You thirsty, Eddie? Let me get you something." He took out the apple juice and I found a clean cup.

While I talked to Jack, Eddie sat in his high chair and glugged down the juice, holding the cup in his two palms. "Somebody killed Ken Buckley because of something that happened fifteen years ago, Jack. I can't believe those two fires happened on the same holiday by chance."

"It sure raises a lot of questions. But nobody died in that fire. Why did someone kill Ken?"

"Especially since setting fire to the house would have been retaliation enough."

"Well, this isn't the day to ask anyone questions in this town. They're all going to the funeral."

"The firemen and their wives were assembling at the firehouse when I got there. Fred took me into Ken's office and let me look at the files. I found an interesting note. The Great Fire started with something burning on the stove. Does that ring a bell?"

He whistled, and Eddie looked up from his juice at the sound. "Sounds like someone was sending a message. A double message."

"I have the name of the family that owned the house. Fred said they moved to another town on Fire Island, west of here. I'm going to look them up. Maybe Joseph and I can trike over there later this afternoon."

"Take a water taxi, Chris. Live it up. It's our last weekend and we can afford it."

I got out the little phone book and looked up Conrad Norris. The town was a few miles west of Blue Harbor. While it might make a pleasurable ride on a bike, Jack was right; we would take a water taxi. I dialed the number and hung up when a man answered. The Norrises were still on Fire Island.

I mopped up Eddie's face, kissing both cheeks as I did so. Then I said to him, "We're going to the ferry to get Joseph. Can you say Joseph?"

He looked at me.

"Joseph? Joseph? Joe?"

No comprehension at all. Oh well, I had tried. I carried him out to the stroller and started for the bay.

It was easy to spot her. Nuns at St. Stephen's Convent still wore the traditional brown habit, albeit updated, and it contrasted with the casual, sometimes colorful, clothing of the handful of other passengers filing off the ferry.

"Here comes Joseph," I said to Eddie. I knelt beside the stroller and pointed toward the group walking up the pier.

When she reached us, we hugged. She was alone, apparently having decided not to bring along a companion.

"Chris, I don't believe this is the little baby I saw a month or two ago." She knelt. "Are you Eddie? You look just like your daddy. I'm Joseph."

He stared at her.

"That's Joseph," I said. "Joseph is coming to stay with us."

He watched as she rose, his face very serious. Then he shouted, "Doe!"

I nearly shrieked with delight. "Yes, that's Joseph," I said.

"Doe!" He pointed. "Doe, Doe."

"Chris, you didn't teach him to say that since last night, did you?"

"I guess I did. I'm as surprised to hear him say it as you are. Every time I tried to get him to say it, he kept looking at me as if I were crazy." I took her bag, which was a soft nylon zipper bag, and stuffed it into the basket at the back of the stroller, and we started walking.

Eddie seemed excited with his new accomplishment. He kept shouting "Doe!" as we walked, sometimes pointing to the sky with his fingers.

"This place is wonderful," Joseph said, as we turned onto a wooden walkway. "And the ferry ride was absolutely invigorating. The breeze was so pure and cool. I can't believe I'm actually somewhere where there aren't any cars."

"You'll get used to it very quickly. The only thing that can run you down here is a bike or tricycle. We have two trikes at our house if you'd like a ride."

"I would just love it. Will we have any time to talk about your murders if we indulge ourselves shamelessly?"

"We'll talk first and do everything else afterwards. I'm so glad you're here, Joseph. It was such short notice I was afraid you wouldn't be able to come."

"I had to cancel a vacation earlier in the summer when we had a severe plumbing problem in the college dormitory and I wasn't able to reschedule it, so I thought I was owed at least a few days. I just love all these little houses and curled-up trees."

"Ours isn't so little. It belongs to Melanie's uncle, and it's quite grand." Joseph had met Mel some time ago, uniting the two friends of my two lives. "We're almost there. This house on the right is where the second murder took place, just out back. The crime-scene tape's probably still up."

"It is."

"And there's Jack."

He came toward us with a big smile, and he and Joseph exchanged their hellos. Jack is always very formal with Joseph. Most of his life experience with nuns was in school, where they both taught and terrorized him. He probably deserved some of the terrorizing, but the feelings they inspired have never quite worn off.

"I thought Eddie'd be fast asleep by now," he said. "It's getting to be nap time."

"I think he's just very excited. You know all the work I did trying to get him to say Joseph? Well, Joseph introduced herself and he's been yelling 'Doe' all the way home."

Eddie gave us two loud examples, complete with finger pointing, and Joseph laughed.

We showed her to her room and the nearby bathroom, and then I got Eddie changed and ready for his nap. He had worn himself out and was only too happy to roll up in a little ball in the crib and close his eyes.

Downstairs, we briefed Joseph on the two homicides. She had come prepared with several pencils and unlined paper and I gave her a book to rest it on while she took notes. She had positioned herself on the sofa so that she was facing the ocean, and she said more than once that she felt overwhelmed by the place, the house, the view, and the ambience. When all our notes had been exhausted in our narrative, we sat back and waited.

"You certainly seem to have latched on to a connection in the dates of the two fires," she said finally. "I gather the earlier one was much more devastating."

"The house was burned to the ground, if what they tell me is true. The Buckley house was saved, although there's smoke and water damage and holes in the second floor and the roof. I would guess in fifteen years the firemen have learned new techniques or bought better equipment. Maybe that's what saved the Buckley house."

"Also, it was larger," Joseph said. "It was two stories. The Norris house was one floor." She looked down at her several pages of notes that included two quick sketches of the houses. "The lawyer, Murchison, I gather no one's spoken to her since the second murder."

"I tried her home number several times last night and again this morning. She doesn't answer. The police chief said that the NYPD had spoken to neighbors who said they hadn't seen her. If she shows up at her apartment, I'm sure there's someone there to pick her up."

"But in the meantime she's disappeared and she's a suspect." She looked down at her notes again. "It looks as though the only new source of information, if they have any, will be the Norrises. Do you know if they're on Fire Island?"

"I checked just after you called from the ferry. A man answered."

Joseph looked at her large, round-faced watch. "Then I'd say that's the place to begin."

18

Jack called for a taxi and we walked down to the bay pier to wait for it.

"I can't believe this is the only means of motorized transportation," Joseph said. "It's as though everyone on this island has rediscovered their legs and their muscles."

"You'll get a chance to use yours when we get back. There are plenty of places to see that we can walk to or trike to. Jack only uses the two-wheeler—I think he thinks a tricycle is an old man's transport—but I enjoy it."

"That must be our taxi now," Joseph said, as a motorboat much smaller than the ferry came toward the pier and turned in to the dock. "I am really getting an education on this trip."

The trip over bumpy waters took less than ten minutes, and when we got to the town where the Norrises lived, the taxi captain directed us to their street.

It was a short walk. The houses were somewhat larger than the ones on the street the Norrises had left behind, and there were some pretty gardens in the front yards. We found the address and walked up to the front door.

The door opened almost immediately in answer to our knock. The woman who greeted us looked to be in her fifties and happily plump. She also seemed more than a little surprised at Joseph's appearance.

"Mrs. Norris," I began, "I'm Chris Bennett and this is

my friend, Sister Joseph, who's visiting me. My husband and I are spending a couple of weeks in Max Margulies's house in Blue Harbor."

"Where the murders were," she said, and I realized everyone on Fire Island must know about them.

"That's right. In fact, we're here to ask you some questions about the fire at your old house in Blue Harbor."

"Why?" she asked with a note of hostility. "We haven't lived there for fifteen years or more."

"I know, but I think the fire at your house may have some bearing on these murders."

She looked at us as though deciding whether to shoo us away or invite us in. Perhaps her curiosity won, because she said, "You'd better come inside," and we followed her to a living room where her husband was sitting with his feet up and reading a book.

We introduced ourselves all around and I thanked them for letting us intrude on their vacation.

"Not much we can tell you about that fire in Blue Harbor," Conrad Norris said. He was wearing jeans and a collared red knit cotton shirt. He had closed the book and put his feet on the floor when we sat down. "We weren't there when it happened and there was nothing left to go back to. We just started looking around for another house and we bought this before the next season."

"This is a lovely house," I said.

"We were lucky it came on the market when it did," his wife said.

"I understand the fire took place on Labor Day."

"That's right," he said. "And we'd left for home that afternoon."

"So you weren't there when the fire started?"

"We were gone," Mrs. Norris said.

"The records showed it was a kitchen fire. How can that be if you weren't at the house?"

They exchanged glances and Mrs. Norris's face looked strained. "I must have left something on the stove."

"Is that what they told you or did you remember it yourself?"

She looked at her husband again. "I didn't remember it, but they investigated and that's what they came up with. So it must have happened that way."

"Did anyone else have the key to your house?" I asked.

"My kids." She looked at her husband. "Where were the kids that day, Connie?"

"They'd left. They got bored pretty quick. They were in their teens then. Lying on the beach doesn't suit teenagers."

I'd heard that before. "What about neighbors? Did you leave a key with the people next door? In case of emergency?"

She looked very pained. "We probably did," she said. "And we had theirs."

It was interesting that she hadn't said a definitive yes, although she was indicating that she might have left her own key. "Can you tell me the name of those neighbors? And where I could find them?"

"They're still there," Conrad Norris said. "The Hersheys. Wilma and Harry. We haven't seen them for years but I don't think they've moved."

"Did they have reason to go into your house when you weren't there?"

Mrs. Norris seemed to be struggling. "We were good neighbors," she said. "We were friendly. If they needed to put a watermelon in my fridge, they were welcome to. If they weren't home, I'd do the same thing, an extra six-pack, a gallon of milk, whatever. They said at the time that they hadn't been in our house. I believed them then and I believe them now. They had no reason to use our stove. It was Labor Day, for heaven's sake. Everyone was either gone or getting ready to go home. They weren't cooking anything in our house."

"So no one could have left the stove on but you." I wanted to hear her say it.

"That's the way it looked. It was my fault."

"Did the insurance pay off?"

"Without any trouble," Conrad said. "It was an accidental fire. It could have happened whether we were there or not."

"Did you know Ken Buckley?" I asked.

"I may have heard the name," she said, and she didn't look quite so uptight any more. "Isn't that the man who was burned to death a few days ago?"

"That's the one. He was shot first."

"You think there's some connection between—?" She looked at me, then at her husband.

"I think there may be. It seems an odd coincidence that the two biggest fires in Blue Harbor both took place on Labor Day. And the fire in the Buckley house started on the stove."

"I hadn't heard that," Conrad said. "That's quite a set of coincidences."

"That's why I'm here," I said.

"What exactly are you thinking?" he asked.

"I wondered whether Ken Buckley could have been involved in the fire in your house and whether someone decided to get even."

They both spoke together, denying the possibility that I was right.

"We didn't know him," she added.

"Maybe he knew the Hersheys."

"Makes no difference," Conrad said. "Everybody in Blue Harbor knew everybody else. You're talking arson. I don't believe that's possible."

"Maybe negligence," I said. "Maybe someone came into your house and turned on the stove and forgot to turn it off."

"Nobody had the key," Norris said firmly. "The house was locked up good and tight. Sandy left something on the stove and after we left, it started a fire. That's it."

The taxi picked us up where it had left us off half an hour earlier. Joseph had said very little to the Norrises, but she had taken notes as we spoke.

"It's amazing to see how they respond," she said, as we bounced over the waves back to Blue Harbor. "Mrs. Norris's face signaled every answer she gave. It's clear she doesn't believe she left anything on that stove. But they certainly defended the Hersheys vigorously."

"I would, too, if they were trusted neighbors. After all, you don't give the key to your house to just anyone."

"I would guess they're next on your list," Joseph said.

"They have to be. There's no one else I can think of that might give me new information except Dodie Murchison, and I don't know where to find her any more than the police do."

"It's interesting to me that these people, the Norrises, didn't throw us out or ask us politely to leave. They were uncomfortable, especially Mrs. Norris, but they talked."

"I've wondered about that myself. She could have closed the door on us at the beginning or said she had nothing more to say at any point, but she didn't. Maybe it's the desire for fresh gossip; the feeling that if she cooperates, she'll learn more about these intriguing murders in a town she once lived in."

"Like the people who put their foot on the brake as they pass an accident on the road when they have no intention of stopping to help. They just want to see it."

I thought it was an apt comparison.

* * *

We set out on the tricycles after lunch and a brief rest in the living room, during which I tried Dodie's home number once again. With each attempt I became more convinced she was involved in one or both of the homicides, but I had no idea how. Would she turn herself in before the weekend was over? What would she do on Monday morning when she was expected at work? I had a feeling she was turning those questions over herself in her own mind, wherever she was.

Joseph and I stopped in front of the house that had been built on the Norrises' lot. I showed her how the bricks from the old chimney had been used around the door and under the windows.

"I understand old brick is quite valuable nowadays," she said. "And here was a supply, absolutely free. I don't blame them for using them."

We cycled the last few feet to the Hersheys' house and I knocked on the door. I hadn't called first, thinking they were so close, we wouldn't have wasted much time if they weren't home.

But they were. A man I estimated to be about ten years older than Conrad Norris opened the door with a friendly "Hiya."

When I'd given my usual explanation of who we were and why we were there, he invited us in to a house reminiscent of Dodie's and Chief La Coste's. Everything was on one floor, but the living room and kitchen had been opened into each other and had become a large, attractive room with new-looking appliances.

Mrs. Hershey was sitting in a chair facing the windows and did not move to rise when we entered. A cane leaned against a table to her right.

"These ladies are asking questions about that fire next door a long time ago, Wilma," Mr. Hershey said to her.

"The Norrises'. I'll never forget that. We were lucky it didn't spread and burn us up, too. There was no wind that day, I remember."

"That was lucky," I said. "Were you and the Norrises good friends?"

"Oh yes, great friends. Harry and Connie used to go down to the bay and go clamming. Remember, Harry? Sweetest clams I ever ate."

"Those were good times," Harry agreed. "Red tide came along; that was the end of the clams. End of an era." He seemed sad.

"Did you keep up with the Norrises?"

"You know, we didn't," Harry said. "We were summer friends. What do they call it? Fair-weather friends. We lived hours apart in the winter. We almost never got together after the summer was over. They moved away, you know. Haven't seen 'em for years."

"But you had the key to their house next door."

"Oh, sure," Wilma said. She adjusted her position in the chair with some difficulty and I wondered how she managed to get down to the ferry. "And they had ours. We were friends and you need someone to have the key in case you lose yours or there's an emergency. The people across the way have ours now."

"Had you been in the Norrises' house the day of the fire?"

"You mean after they left? No. Why would we?"

"I just wondered about the stove in their kitchen."

"That was too bad, wasn't it? Sandy must've left it on and forgot all about it."

"I thought maybe you went in there for something and used the stove that day after the Norrises left."

"We weren't in that house," her husband said. "I'll swear to that in a court of law. And we never gave the key to anybody."

"Did you know Ken Buckley?" I addressed both of them.

"Knew him and liked him," Harry said.

"The funeral's today."

"It's hard for the wife to get around. We decided to send flowers instead."

"How did you come to know Ken?"

"He was always a very friendly guy. Even after he became chief, he and a couple of firemen would come around collecting for the fire department. I really got to know him when I was a volunteer fireman, but that was a long time ago. I developed some heart problems and the doc said I should give it up."

"Was Ken part of the group that responded to the alarm for the Norrises' house?"

"Couldn't tell ya," Harry said. "There were so goddamn many—excuse me, Sister, I didn't mean to offend—there were so many firemen from so many towns, I couldn't tell ya who was there and who wasn't."

"It was some mess," his wife said. "Water all over the place. Everything was mud the next day. I never saw anything like it. When they ran out of freshwater, they had to pump it out of the sea. Nothing worse than salt water."

"Did you turn in the alarm?" I asked.

"Yes, but other people did, too. You could really see those flames from out front."

"What time was the fire?" It was the first question Joseph had asked.

The Hersheys looked at each other. "Evening," Harry said. "I couldn't tell you the exact time."

"The Norrises left their house in the afternoon. It seems like a long time for something to be on the stove before the fire broke out."

"Couldn't tell ya anything about it. They looked into

it. That's what they said happened. Something on the stove burned out."

"Do you know anyone named Frisch?" I asked.

"I don't," Wilma said. "You, Harry?"

"Never heard the name in my life."

"You know anyone named Tina?"

They shook their heads. I looked over at Joseph.

"I have no other questions," she said. She stood and walked to the windows. "This is such a lovely vacation spot. I've heard about Fire Island for years and seen that skinny strip of land just below Long Island, but I never imagined it to be like this. You're very lucky to have a home here."

"Well, we love it," Wilma said. "I haven't been able to walk good for almost ten years, but I've got a little motorized scooter I get around on and Harry helps out with groceries. When we first moved here, you had to bring everything from the mainland."

"You mean, you carried your food with you?" Joseph asked.

"Oh, yes. That's the way it was back then. We'd bring it over in cartons and coldpacks and load it on wagons when we got off the ferry. We still bring things out with us, but there's no panic if you run out."

We finished up our visit soon after that and pedaled back to our house. Jack was in the living room reading one of his law books, and we sat on the front deck and talked.

"I love to hear them recall the good old days," Joseph said. "The bay had the sweetest clams till the red tide came. What do you think, Chris? Are we closer to an answer?"

"I'm troubled," I admitted. "The Norrises left in the afternoon, the fire started in the evening. Presumably it took all those hours for the fire to start. I suppose that's possible."

"But you're troubled. And I am, too. I'm also troubled by Tina Frisch's part in all this. No one seems to have heard of her."

"But she was at the fire, she was hiding her identity, she denied having been there, and she had a fireman's coat that she hid at Chief La Coste's house." I had briefed Joseph on all the relevant figures in our first conversation. "And it certainly looks as though Tina murdered Ken Buckley and lost her life for it."

"It does look that way, but I'm not happy with that solution. Who would avenge Ken Buckley's death?"

"His wife, but she wasn't on the island Wednesday night. She was at the wake for her husband."

"Then who else?" she asked rhetorically. "And then there's Attorney Murchison. We believe she was doing legal work for Ken Buckley and it sounds as though she may have been involved with him in more intimate ways as well. An estate attorney that he met on the beach and hired to do legal work for him. On the face of it, it seems rather preposterous."

"I agree."

"I would like to meet your Chief La Coste. Not that I'll be able to extract anything new from him, but he sounds like a very interesting person. Living on this island in the winter must be quite an experience."

"We can go over later in the afternoon. I worry that he may take a nap after lunch and I don't want to disturb him. As robust as he seems to be, I'm sure he needs a lot more sleep than we do. But we could walk down the street and take a look at the second crime scene."

"That sounds like a good idea. And happily, this crime scene will not have a body on the premises." She was referring to a time not so long ago when we had made a terrible discovery together.

I told Jack where he could find us, and we walked over to the Kleins' house.

19

Someone was coming down the ramp with two suit-cases on a wagon as we approached. It was one of the girls I had only said hello to. She looked ready to embark on a long trip and I realized this was the last day of their season, the day they cleaned up, packed up, and went home for the start of fall. Today their summer was truly over.

Kyle was helping her. He pulled the wagon and the girl clutched a stuffed bear as though she were a child in need of security, which, perhaps, was not a bad description of how she felt.

"Hi, Chris," Kyle called. "Coming to see me?"

"Coming to look at where it happened."

"Don't touch anything, OK? Chief Springer said there was no one to leave to guard the area, but they might have to come back and do more work there."

"I'll be careful."

"I'll be back soon if you feel like talking."

"Maybe we'll see you."

He pulled the wagon toward the bay while the girl kept a hand on the suitcases. Joseph and I walked around the right side of the big house to the yellow crime scene tape, which enclosed not just the gate to the crawl space but also a section of grass outside it.

"She was found in there," I said, pointing. "Near or on

top of the bicycle." I couldn't see the bicycle and thought the police had probably taken it with them.

"So the body was hidden."

"For many hours. Possibly twelve. The autopsy should give us some idea."

There wasn't much to see. The grass outside the crawl space was weedy and scraggly, beaten down by lots of feet, suffering from a lack of water and fertilizer. Besides those of the occupants of the house, there must have been several additional pairs of feet yesterday, heavy men's feet in heavy shoes.

"The bike wasn't on top of her," Joseph said.

"I don't think so. I think she was on top of the bike."

"So it would appear that she came back from her bike ride and someone was waiting in the dark for her. She put the bike away, he killed her, and then he stuffed her body in the crawl space."

"Or she could have met him on her ride. Then she might have walked her bike home with him, not suspecting he intended to kill her."

Joseph looked thoughtful. "Both are possible. She knew him, she didn't know him."

"He waited for her, he ran into her by accident."

Joseph laughed. "We aren't doing very well, are we?"

I walked around to the back of the house. There was a door to the deck from what must be the kitchen. As I looked up at the door, it opened and Danielle came out on the deck.

"Chris?"

"Hi. I'm just looking at the place where it happened."

"There isn't much to see. They took the bicycle. I'm leaving in a little while. I was going to go this morning, but I didn't want to get on a ferry with all the people going to the funeral. So I decided to wait for afternoon. Want to come inside?"

"Sure. I have a friend with me."

The three of us sat at the kitchen table. Danielle looked awful. "I'm just waiting for Kyle to bring back the wagon and then I'll go," she said. "My boyfriend is upstairs stripping the beds and I'm cleaning out the fridge. The Kleins are coming tonight if you want to talk to them. I don't know what they can tell you."

"I don't know, either."

"That lawyer's missing, isn't she?"

"It appears so."

"How could a woman have killed Tina? It's crazy."

"Danielle, Jack and I are staying till Sunday. We'll probably leave right after lunch. If you think of anything, if you hear anything, will you call? You can reach us at home Sunday night."

"I will. But there isn't anything. I've told you everything I know."

"I need to connect Tina to Ken Buckley or his wife." I didn't say anything about the mysterious "Uncle Bill" of Chief La Coste's story because it sounded so absurd.

"I'll call if I think of anything."

We didn't wait for Kyle. Danielle said he wasn't leaving till the Kleins came. Devoted to the water, he wanted one last shot at the waves and the shells before leaving summer behind.

Back at the house, Eddie had just awakened. He was warm and weepy, and I held him for a while until he was fully awake. A pretzel cheered him up and he gave Joseph a smile and said her name a couple of times to show he hadn't forgotten. I put him in the stroller and we walked over to the Buckley house.

Ida Bloom was at the funeral and the doors were locked, so we walked around the house as I pointed out to Joseph where the rooms were and where I was standing when Tina pushed her way through the crowd with the fireman's coat over her.

From there we walked over to Chief La Coste's little house. He opened the door and beamed at Eddie. "So you came back to me, you little cutie," he said, ruffling Eddie's curls. "How are you, Chris? I see you've got a friend with you."

I introduced Joseph and we went inside. The chief gave Eddie a cookie, which probably made him Eddie's friend for life. Then he said, "You don't know how much I wanted to be at that funeral. I called Eve and she said, 'Bernie, just stay put. It's hard on all of us. I'd never forgive myself if something happened to you.' She's a good woman. So I stayed here, and I can't stop thinkin' about that wonderful friend I'll never see again. All those conversations, all those good times, gone forever."

"What do you do for company in the winter, Chief?" I asked. We had sat in the living room and I was hoping Eddie would be content in his stroller. I didn't want to let him crawl around on the chief's floor.

"There's about twenty of us families that stay here all year round and we look after each other. We got a chain phone system going. Someone calls me in the morning to see how I'm doin' and I call someone else. We're a real community. We get to keep cars here, you know, after the summer's over. I give my grocery list to some folks and they drive over the causeway from Robert Moses State Park to the mainland and deliver my stuff as right as rain. And I take my walks. Gotta stay fit, you know."

"The last of the summer people are on their way back today. It'll be pretty empty without them."

"That's how I like it best. The deer'll make their way in from the park, lookin' for something to eat. They get pretty hungry in the winter, poor things."

He seemed very low today and I couldn't blame him. I

hoped he would get through the winter, that his spirits would recover.

"Are they tame?" I asked.

"Pretty tame. Some of them eat right outta your hand. Course they're not very friendly to grass and flowers." He smiled, then turned to Eddie and made faces at him. "I did what you told me to, Chris," he said finally. "I called Curt and told him I had the turnout coat. He came by early and picked it up, said maybe they could remove the ink and find the name underneath. I thought indelible meant you couldn't do that, but who knows? Seems like they can do almost anything nowadays."

"We visited the Hersheys a little while ago," I said.

"Hershey, Hershey . . ."

"The people who live next door to where the big fire was."

"Oh yes, Hershey. Harry's his name. She's got some trouble walkin' these last years."

"Those are the ones."

"Yeah, I guess they'll never forget it either."

"Were you there to see the fire?"

"Can't keep me away from a fire, I'll tell ya. I walked over, sure. They said you could see the flames at the western end of the island."

"Any chance it was arson, Chief?"

He looked at me with sharp eyes. "What makes you ask that? The report said Mrs. Norris left something on the stove."

Joseph answered. "It seems strange to us that the Norrises left something on the stove in the afternoon and the fire started hours later."

"Happens all the time. Most fires around here are kitchen fires. Barbecue fires." He shrugged. "Nothin' unusual about that."

"Who was chief at that time?" I asked.

"Well, let's see. That was prob'ly Chief Rutledge, but I can tell you he wasn't there. In those days, we had the big picnic around noon, after all the parades ended, and George Rutledge, he got on the ferry just as soon as the picnic was over. Hadda be at work Tuesday morning so he left."

"Did someone stand in for him?"

"I kinda recollect Ken Buckley was acting chief that day. Ken always stayed on till the end of the week."

Eddie had been watching him very intently. Now he pointed to Joseph and said, "Doe." We laughed and explained it to the chief, who started a conversation with Eddie.

I knew that he was finished talking to us about the fire. He didn't want to talk about any of the things that were relevant to the murders. I could understand it in a way. Ken Buckley had been a friend and a source of companionship. Tina Frisch had been a young girl with most of her life ahead of her. And arson was a dirty word to those in the fire-fighting service.

We talked about lighter things for a while and left when Eddie got restless. Instead of walking back to the house, I continued toward the beach.

"This is where he goes at night," I told Joseph. "I think he carries a lightweight chair with him and sets it up facing the ocean. And he smokes a cigarette."

"That sounds very lovely to me. He's turned a vice into an innocent pleasure. I must say, I'm sure a place like this gets in your blood, but I can't imagine enjoying such isolation in the winter, not to mention the weather. The wind must be unbearable."

"There's no easy explanation for love."

I took Eddie out of the stroller and walked onto the dune, carrying him. "There's our house. It's really quite close."

"And the deer come from where?"

"There are parks at both ends of the island, Robert Moses State Park at the western end and a bunch of parks in the east. Altogether, the deer have twenty-five miles of park. The humans have only seven miles at the western end of the island."

"Twenty-five miles of park," Joseph said. "I suppose there must be a lot of deer."

I agreed. I put Eddie back in his stroller and we took the long way home, through the streets.

It was late afternoon by the time we got back. Considering that Joseph had arrived only this morning, we had certainly been around. Jack was just coming back from a swim in the pool, rather a cool day for that, but I'm sure he felt as I did: if you didn't do it now, you'd wait a year for the next opportunity.

I told him what Chief La Coste had reluctantly admitted, that Ken Buckley was acting fire chief the night of the Great Fire.

"So we know he was there," Jack said. "Anyone mind if I shower right away?"

We shooed him off but he stopped on the way to the stairs. "You ladies see the extra key?"

I looked over at the board in the kitchen where the keys had hung since our arrival and saw that the extra set was gone. I felt the pockets of my shorts. I got my handbag and opened it on the kitchen table, feeling around the bottom and sides without luck. "I don't seem to have them. I don't remember taking them off the board."

"Did you give them to anyone?" Joseph asked.

"No, of course not. Who would I give them to?"

"That's weird," Jack said. "I hope they turn up before we leave."

"Did Kyle drop by? We saw him just for a minute when

we went to look at the crime scene. He was walking one of the girls down to the ferry but we didn't wait for him to come back."

"Haven't seen anyone," Jack said.

"This is very creepy." It gave me an uncomfortable feeling. If we locked up tonight, would we be safe? "Take a shower. We'll look later."

A moment later the phone rang. We picked up at the same time and I recognized Curt Springer's voice. I hung up and let Jack take the call.

Jack came downstairs twenty minutes later looking freshly dressed, his hair still damp and forming ringlets as I watched it. "That was Springer. They've matched prints from the house Dodie Murchison stayed in with prints on the bicycle at Tina's place."

"Dodie touched the bicycle?"

"Looks like it. He said there was a great set of her whole hand on one of the handlebars, on the rubber cover on the handlebar."

"I gather he hasn't found her."

"Not yet, but he and the sheriff want her for questioning. Real bad."

"And she must know it. But she's got to turn herself in sometime soon. Monday is a workday."

"She'll do what's right."

Joseph looked at her watch. "If you nice people will excuse me, it's five o'clock."

Five o'clock was evening prayer time at St. Stephen's. "May I join you, Joseph?"

"I'd be happy if you would. Let's go out on the front deck."

"See you ladies later. Eddie and I are going to look for those keys."

I grabbed a couple of pillows and took them outside.

We knelt side by side along the railing facing the sea. To our right the sun was preparing to set in the west; ahead of us and to the left the great Atlantic stretched south and east to places I had never been but that someday might be within reach. I had not prayed with the nuns of St. Stephen's for three years, yet the words came as easily as if I had spoken them the thousand and some times since the day I left. When we sang, I heard Joseph's clear, strong voice leading the way as she had led and assisted me in the years I spent as a guest, a novice, and a nun in the convent. My own voice hardly matched hers in color and intensity. I have the greatest difficulty carrying a tune but I sing with great enthusiasm and pleasure.

It was a wonderful half hour, perhaps the best of the two weeks we had spent in this magnificent house. As we prayed and recited and sang, I thought of other times, of my great affection and admiration for Joseph, of my own good fortune in being here with these people that formed my family.

When we were finished, I remained on my knees looking out to sea. After a few moments, I realized that Joseph had taken her pillow and walked away. I took a deep breath of the salt-air breeze and stood up.

Joseph was standing in the rounded area where the deck wrapped around from the front to the far side of the house. I walked over. She was looking toward the west.

"We should see a fine sunset tonight," she said.

"Yes, it's very clear. We've been treated to a lot of them these past two weeks."

"And tomorrow morning I'll see the sunrise from where we've just been kneeling."

"I think you will."

"Worth the trip even if I hadn't had the chance to see you and your family."

We went inside where Jack was sitting at the kitchen

table talking to Kyle. Kyle was wet and sandy from his last dip in the ocean, a little uncomfortable about the puddles he was leaving on our kitchen floor. I assured him we intended to take care of the cleanup tomorrow and not to worry.

"Danielle's gone," he said. "I don't think she'll ever set foot on Fire Island again."

"I can't blame her," I said. "Have the Kleins arrived?"

"They're here. When they started going over the house and making a note of every missing chip of paint, I figured it was time for me to take a swim."

"I'm sure renting out a house has its problems."

"Well, we weren't the neatest group. But we paid for a cleaning service to come in next week. You find anything out yet? About Tina?"

"Not too much," Jack said. "You think of anything that can help us?"

"Danielle gave me this. She found it right after Chris left this afternoon. She said to give it to you." He opened the zipper bag that I had assumed held his snorkeling gear—and maybe it did—and pulled out a plastic bag with an upscale Manhattan supermarket's name on it. "It's a notebook. It's Tina's."

"Where'd Danielle find it?"

"In the refrigerator, if you can believe it. Looks like Tina didn't want anyone to find it. Danielle said she was cleaning out the shelves and this was under a carton of eggs."

Jack had opened it and was turning pages. "Looks very interesting, Kyle. I appreciate your turning this over." He closed it and rested his hand on it. "We have your address and phone number, don't we?"

"Yeah, I gave it to Chris." He stood. "I guess it's good-bye." He reached out a big hand and shook each of ours.

I couldn't help thinking as he gripped my hand that

these were hands that could do a lot of damage, and I immediately felt guilty for thinking so. He had liked Tina. It had been she who seemed not to want a relationship. There was no reason to believe he would do injury to her.

20

After Kyle left, Jack grabbed the mop from the utility closet and went over the puddles our guest had left behind. He laughed as he did it. "No wonder folks with nice houses don't want to rent them out. Forget the paint chips. There must be salt water and sand on every floor and every chair in that house."

"What's in the notebook?" I asked.

"Lots of good stuff. Looks like she kept a kind of diary of her search."

"I'm torn," I admitted. "Eddie needs his supper and bath and I can't wait to see what's in that notebook."

Joseph was all smiles. "I'm glad to hear motherhood hasn't taken you over completely. I'll resist temptation till Eddie is safely in his crib."

"I knew I could count on you," I said, lifting my little one off the floor with a swoop and a kiss.

"OK, I'm outvoted." Jack put the notebook back in its plastic bag and dropped it on the table. "I'll start getting things ready for dinner so we'll have a little time before the Jorgensens come."

We had invited them to meet Joseph and join us for spareribs. And until we had read every word of the notebook, I had no intention of sharing its contents with anyone. Jack had put together his best barbecue sauce during the day. I knew this because I smelled it when we returned from one of our jaunts. "OK, Eddie," I said, my eye on the precious package, "it's bath and suppertime. How does that sound to you?" I gave him a big kiss and we got started.

Joseph was more interested in the almost ten-month-old Eddie than she had been in the little baby. She was clearly pleased that he said her name, and she joined in the good-night kisses when he was ready for bed. I took him upstairs and read to him from a picture book with hard cardboard pages, showing him the pictures and talking to him about them. When he started looking drowsy, I put him in his crib. Three little fingers went right into his mouth and he closed his eyes. I dashed downstairs.

Jack had cleaned and cut the vegetables, made his wonderful blue cheese dip, and was sitting at the kitchen table with Joseph, the notebook untouched between them.

"You are the two most honorable people I know," I said. "Are we going to look now?"

"You bet." Jack slipped it out of the bag. It was an ordinary spiral notebook with a soft cover picturing some rock star unknown to me standing in front of a microphone, holding a guitar and singing his heart out. Jack opened the cover, and inside was a sticker like those you get in the mail from organizations that want donations. On it was Tina's name and address.

The pages were written mostly in blue ballpoint—Jack flipped through them before turning back to the beginning—but occasionally in pencil or some other color of ink. Tina had grabbed whatever was near to make her notes.

"Well, here's the beginning. No date." He began to read.

" 'I know he was my father. Mom always said no but I believe Bill was my father. I remember the last time I saw him, just an ordinary visit. Afterwards I remember asking Mom why he didn't come around anymore. She said she didn't know and for a long time I didn't believe her. But I believe her now. He had simply disappeared. I want to find him. I want to know the truth. And I will.

" 'A group of us will rent a house on Fire Island. I volunteered to do the dirty work so I could get a place in or near the town of Blue Harbor. That's where Bill told Mom he was going the last time he came to see us.'

"There are a lot of short notes here," Jack said. "She visited Blue Harbor, she mentions Honey Quinn, the realtor, the Kleins' house, a couple of other houses. Let's see. This must be her first weekend out here." He moved his finger down the page.

" 'Walked around. Took a swim. Talked to a neighbor who's lived here over twenty years. Said I should see an old man named La Coste. Will look him up next time.

" 'Found La Coste. He's really old, over ninety. Asked him about deaths in Blue Harbor fifteen or so years ago. Says he doesn't remember any. Went to police station. Cop named Springer. Wasn't here when Bill disappeared. Doesn't like "fishing expeditions" into his files but said maybe next time I come he'll let me look. Bernie La Coste says he'll look in the files for me.' "

"Was Tina out here all summer?" Joseph asked.

"No. The group, there were about ten of them, shared the house. They alternated weekends so that about five were out here every weekend. Half of them came for the Fourth of July and the other half for Labor Day. Most of them took their vacations out here for a week or two. Tina took the weeks before and after Labor Day, the way we did."

"So Tina had only a small number of weekends to work on her project."

"That's the way it looks," Jack said.

"Sorry for the interruption. Please go on."

" 'Bernie La Coste saw the police files! Made a list of several years of fights and disturbances when I got back. No one named Bill or Will or William. No Jamieson at all. No one killed. No one even badly hurt. No drownings. No boating accidents. Where is he? Nobody seems to be hiding anything. Could he have come and gone and *then* disappeared?

" 'Housemates worried that I don't join in the "fun." I do but they expect more. Kyle very sweet. I like him but can't spend all my time with him and don't feel like explaining what I'm doing. Have to keep looking. Maybe get together in the winter.

" 'Talked to a couple of people where fights took place. They don't even remember them so how important could they have been?

" 'What else is there? Bernie talked about big fire about that time if he has his dates right. But house was empty. Next time.

" 'Not much time left. It poured two weeks ago. Stayed home. Nice weather this weekend. House that burned down in Bernie's "Great Fire" is really gone. Talked to people across the street. Said nothing was left except chimney. Same as Bernie said. Lots of firemen. Lots of water. Everything a mess afterward. Could Bill have been there? *Could he have set fire?*

" 'Went to firehouse. Like a sitcom. Old guys sit around playing cards and pool. Won't let me look at their files.' "

"That's interesting," I interrupted. "When I was down there this morning, Fred invited me into the chief's office. He said their files were open to the public."

"Maybe they removed something damaging after Buckley died," Jack suggested.

"You're talking about a conspiracy. With a lot of people involved. Maybe they just didn't want Tina poking around. Maybe the person she talked to didn't feel he had the authority to let her look. Or was too lazy to show her the files."

Jack turned a page.

" 'This is a mess. I'll never find out what happened. Maybe he just met a girl and took her to California. Maybe he's not my father after all. Maybe he and Mom had a fight and they split up. But she told me he was going to Fire Island. She said he was going to Blue Harbor. What if he went swimming and drowned and got washed out to sea? He was a daytripper. No one knew who he was. There isn't much to check anymore. If I don't find out the truth on my vacation, it's all over. I think he drowned. I think he's dead. I think he's in California.' "

"Poor thing," Joseph said. "This search really consumed her. If this man was really her father, someone should have told her."

"He may not have been," Jack said. "It could have been a fantasy that wouldn't let go." He looked down at the page.

" 'This is it. Got here this afternoon (Sunday). The alternate gang hadn't left yet. Had to wait to get into my bedroom. They're complete slobs. They don't even blow the dust away. What a mess.

" 'Saw Bernie. He just likes to talk. Sat on his deck and listened. Said Polly Adler used to live on Fire Island. Then he talked about the hurricane of 'thirty-eight. Must have been awful. Houses swept into the sea. Roofs lifted off. Walls collapsed.

" 'Finally I asked him if I could talk to a fireman about the Great Fire. He said see Chief Buckley. Stopped at Chief Buckley's house on the way back. No one home.

" 'Tried the firehouse this morning. No one knows where he is. Maybe off island. Sure to come back for Labor Day.

" 'Tried the firehouse again. No Buckley. Not at home either.

" 'Success! Talked to Chief Buckley today. Says he remembers the Great Fire very well. Says there isn't much to tell but why don't I come over on Labor Day? There's some party on the beach and we can talk in his house. Hope he doesn't come on to me. He's got to be fifty and I like Kyle better.

" 'Have to organize my thoughts. When was fire? (Date and time) Anyone hurt? Whose house? Who was home? Names, addresses. Was it arson? Accident? Whose fault? Why can't I think of anything else to ask?

" 'Labor Day. This is it. They're setting up tents on the beach. Ran into Bernie.' "

Jack looked up. "That's all."

"It ends just like that?" I said.

"Just like that." He flipped pages but they were all empty.

"It's just like stepping off a cliff. My heart is pounding. I feel as if I were the one who was going to the Buckley house."

"She must have been too upset when she came back to write anything," Joseph said.

"Or too busy trying to hide the coat she picked up," Jack said. "She had to ink out what was probably Buckley's name and get it out of the house before the police came to question her. Once she saw Chris, she knew she was in trouble."

"But we still don't know what happened," I said. "She never mentions a weapon. We don't know whether she went to his house with or without the gun that killed him. And I have to say, if he was waiting for her in bed without any clothes on, it looks as though he, at least, had something more planned than a question-answer session."

"She says in the book that she hopes not," Joseph said. "Although I guess she could have written that to protect herself."

"Then why write anything?" I was beside myself with disappointment. "Why even mention she was going to his house?"

"I gotta tell you, I owe Bernie La Coste a big apology," Jack said. "Remember what I said about his tale about 'Uncle Bill'?"

"You're forgiven," I said. "The way he told it, it sounded like the whole thing was made up." I turned to Joseph. "It was really hard to take Chief La Coste's story seriously, but it's exactly what Tina has in her book."

"I feel very sorry for the poor child," she said.

"Well, ladies, it looks like we have as many unanswered questions as we had before and we have guests coming in a little while. I think we can be pretty sure Tina got back across the street in a panic. I remember what you said, Chris, about when you followed her. She came to a fence she couldn't scale and she was practically screaming with frustration."

"That's right. Whether she killed Ken or found him dead or just walked into the house and found the kitchen on fire, it must have really panicked her. And then when she was trying to slip away without anyone seeing her, I recognized her under the coat and started to follow her home."

Joseph stood up. "I'm waiting for my assignment. Set the table? Carry food somewhere? Stir something? I'm at your service."

Jack closed the notebook and slid it back into the plastic bag. "Dinner first, homicide later. Here we go."

It was a wonderful evening and the three of us almost forgot what had riveted us at the kitchen table earlier. The Jorgensens brought an excellent bottle of wine—well, Jack said it was excellent; my taste buds still haven't matured— and we never seemed to run out of conversation.

Before we ate, I talked to Al privately for a few minutes and said I had come to believe that his friend whose daughter had been involved with Ken Buckley probably had no part in his death, and Al said he'd never thought he did. He took Joseph and me by the arms and walked us along the beach heading west, as he and I had walked together a few nights earlier. The last of the sun was still streaking the clouds with a vibrant pink, and Joseph exclaimed her pleasure.

I looked around for the solitary man on his beach chair, for the glow of a cigarette on the dune, but there was nothing. "I don't see Chief La Coste tonight," I said to Al.

"He's probably gone to bed early. He went to the funeral, didn't he?"

"No, he didn't. He said Eve told him not to come because he might get too upset."

"Good advice. Eve's a wonderful woman. Ken was lucky to have her."

I felt uncomfortable. Bernie La Coste was too old not to worry about. But Al was talking about other things, showing Joseph the nighttime vista. There were the lights of Fire Island, stretching for miles. He named the towns in order, giving each a brief description. He showed us where the tide had reached the last time it came in He was voluble and easygoing, and when we finally turned around and walked east again, I was surprised how far we had come.

"And down at the eastern end of the island," he said, pointing ahead of us, "is the preserve, twenty-five miles set aside for the deer. The deer, in this case, get three times the land that the people get." He kept talking, describing what Joseph would not have time to see on this very brief visit. "Yes, everything's changed," he said nostalgically. "Those ferries they run nowadays? Before they got those going, they used to use old rum-runners from the Twenties. Took forever to cross the bay and only held twenty, twenty-five people. These new ones hold a hundred and twenty and only take half an hour. But you know that if you took one out."

It was cool and breezy. There were no evening swimmers and few people sitting on the beach. Joseph had decided to go home tomorrow. I had offered to take her to the Catholic church for mass tomorrow morning and again on Sunday, but I think when she saw the price of the water taxi, seven dollars each round trip, she decided against it. I was happy to pay, but she said it was better if she returned on Saturday and attended mass Sunday morning at St. Stephen's. Joseph is a very decisive person, and I'm sure she knew that my offer was genuine, so I did not press her.

Jack's dinner was marvelous and the wine struck him as a perfect accompaniment. Joseph offered a toast to all of us, and I felt very happy that she had been able to come, to share our vacation home, to eat well and talk to pleasant people.

Before the evening was over, I asked the Jorgensens if they had somehow come into possession of our second set of house keys.

"We have our own set," Marti said. "Have you misplaced yours?"

"They disappeared from the board in the kitchen and we haven't been able to find them. I didn't really think you had them, but I don't know who else to ask."

"Well, you know keys. They have a habit of getting lost and turning up in the strangest places."

"Maybe we'll find them tomorrow when we clean up."

"I'll keep a good watch on the house, Chris. Al's going back home on Sunday but I'll stay for a while. It's always so nice and quiet when the summer people leave."

But I couldn't help wondering about the keys. Could someone have come in when we weren't home and snatched them? Could it have been Kyle?

After the Jorgensens left and we were all in the kitchen cleaning up, I mentioned to Jack that Chief La Coste hadn't been sitting in his usual spot on the beach.

"Want me to run over and check?" he asked.

"It wouldn't be a bad idea. Take the bike and I'll finish up the dishes."

"*We'll* finish up," Joseph said.

Jack needed no more encouragement. I filled the dishwasher and got started on the few pots and the dishes that we preferred to do by hand.

"A wonderful evening," Joseph said. "I never imagined such luxury."

"You must be exhausted. Why don't you go up to bed so you don't miss your sunrise?"

She hesitated, but this time I pushed and she went off to bed. Jack took longer than I expected and I began to worry. What if the chief had become ill? Even avoiding the funeral would not keep him from thinking about the terrible events of the last few days.

But Jack returned eventually, and in good spirits. "He says he dozed off after dinner and then it was too cool to go to the beach. I joined him for a brandy and did a lot of listening."

"I'm glad you went."

"Me, too." He kissed me. "It was damn good brandy."

21

When I came downstairs with Eddie the next morning, Joseph and Jack were fixing a sumptuous breakfast. While I fed Eddie, or at least tried to guide the food into his mouth, Joseph described the sunrise with great enthusiasm.

"I don't remember the last time I saw the sun rise over the ocean," she said. "It was just wonderful. Even without my usual sleep, I feel energetic."

We ate heartily, Tina's notebook on the table.

"You know I have to turn that over to Curt Springer," Jack said.

"It'll probably just reinforce his theory that Tina killed Ken, and Dodie killed Tina."

"Tina may well have killed Ken," Jack said. "What do you think, Sister Joseph? You haven't expressed many opinions on our double homicide."

Joseph laughed. "And it's presumably the reason for my visit. Well, I've been accumulating facts and opinions, and I do have a few things on my mind. First, it's not out of the question that Tina murdered Mr. Buckley. But if she did, I would have to assume that she did not walk into his bedroom, put a bullet in the back of his head, and walk out, whether she set fire to the house or not. No one has come up with the slightest motive for her to kill him, including her notebook. So we would have to imagine that she had a conversation with him in which he disclosed something quite terrible to her, so terrible that she used the gun she had brought along just in case."

"So what's the motive?" I asked.

"Since, according to Tina's own notebook, she did not find any indication that 'Uncle Bill' was killed in a fight, drowned in the ocean, fell down dead of a heart attack or stroke or any other event in the police file, it would have to be something that Mr. Buckley was himself involved in or had direct knowledge of. Now, it's rather too unlikely that Buckley himself killed 'Uncle Bill.' It really stretches the imagination to think that Tina stumbled on the killer quite by chance when looking into the Great Fire. It's more likely that Bill's disappearance is connected with that fire, and that Buckley knew about it because, as a fireman, he was personally involved in it."

"I don't mean to break your train of thought," Jack said, "but it's been nagging at me that there's one person we haven't talked to who might have direct knowledge of that fire, the police chief at that time, Jerry O'Donnell."

"He's in Key West, I think," I said.

"I can do better than that. Curt gave me his phone number on one of my visits and I just haven't thought about calling him. How's about now?"

"I think you should," Joseph said.

Jack dialed, as I worried about the phone bill we were leaving behind. Mel would have to get it for us so we could—

"Yes, I'm looking for Jerry O'Donnell . . . Chief O'Donnell," Jack began, explaining the who and what of his phone call.

We sat back and listened, although it sounded as though Jack wasn't getting very much from the retired policeman. There was more small talk than substantive conversation, but when Jack hung up, he looked like someone who had just made chief of detectives.

"O'Donnell had the day off. Someone in his wife's family got married that day, and he didn't get back till late Tuesday to see the ashes."

"Then we haven't missed anything from him," Joseph said.

"There was one titillating bit of information," Jack said, his lips curling in a smile. "O'Donnell said that when he was away from Fire Island, he always appointed someone to stand in for him. Usually it was the fire chief—who's dead now by the way; he died a couple of years ago—but the fire chief turned him down that day because of the picnic, and he was going home that afternoon. So he got someone else. He picked Ken Buckley."

There was a collective "Ahh" from Joseph and me, and Eddie, sitting on the floor, looked up and pointed at Joseph, calling, "Doe, Doe," as though he wanted to join in the fun.

When we finished laughing, I said, "This is really very neat. Whether the firemen were called or the police were called, Ken Buckley would be there. And I bet he wrote up the police file on the Great Fire."

"Which we've never seen," Jack reminded us. "All we know about that file is what Chief La Coste told Tina and Tina put in her book. Which wasn't much."

"If Ken Buckley was trying to hide something," Joseph said, "I doubt whether the police file would tell us much."

"But what are we talking about? Did Tina's Uncle Bill burn down the Norrises' house? And if he did, what happened to him? And why would he do it?" I turned to Jack. "I wish we could find Dodie Murchison. Maybe Tina told her something she didn't write in her notebook."

I got up and dialed the number yet again with no success. This time I waited for the machine to answer and I left a message: "Dodie, this is Chris Bennett Brooks. Please talk to us. We'll be in Blue Harbor till Sunday afternoon, then at our home." I dictated the numbers, although I was sure I had already left them yesterday.

"Sister Joseph, I have to apologize. I interrupted you when I called Jerry O'Donnell. You were telling us what you've come up with, and I hope you can still remember what you were going to say."

"Yes, absolutely. Don't worry about interruptions, Jack. Each one seems to add something important, and that call was no exception. I agree that it would be nice if you heard from Attorney Murchison, but it would be especially nice if it turns out she didn't murder Tina. Because if she murdered Tina, it's simply an angry lover getting revenge. If someone else murdered Tina, the reason may lie in what happened at the Great Fire, and that's what interests me. I can't tell you who Uncle Bill is or whether he was Tina's father, as she hoped he was. But I think something happened that night in the Norrises' house that led all these years later to Tina spending the summer across the street and to the death of Ken Buckley. More than that, I believe there are people here on Fire Island, including the Hersheys, who know exactly what happened and who have kept it secret all these years."

"Because they were involved in it?" I asked.

"Possibly. Possibly because withholding information is a crime and they have reasons why they can't tell what they know. Possibly because they were involved in some way in whatever happened. And I don't think Mrs. Norris left a pot of stew on the stove when they went home. And she doesn't think so, either."

"I see why you dash up to St. Stephen's whenever you

need help," Jack said. "I like the way you think, Sister Joseph. I like the way you look at things."

"This has been a new and really very gratifying experience. I was able to look at the faces of those who had direct knowledge, to see their discomfort, to observe their dodging the truth or how they explained away facts that displeased them." She turned to me. "I see why doing this kind of work holds your interest. It certainly complements the teaching of poetry."

"It's different," I admitted. "And it's very satisfying. I gather from what you've said that you think some of the people we spoke to yesterday were lying to us."

"Oh, yes. And it comes down to your lost keys, Chris."

"The keys. I don't—"

"You'll see when you think about it. People don't always lie to keep back the truth. Think about the photos we saw at the Hersheys', their children now grown up and married. Recall the way people answered your questions or how they didn't."

"If Dodie Murchison didn't kill Tina in a fit of jealousy, what do you think her part in all this is? Why did she go to see Tina the night that Tina was killed?"

"Perhaps just to find out what Tina knew. You told Murchison that you saw Tina leaving the Buckley premises. Maybe Murchison just wanted to check it out for herself, to see if Tina would confirm that she was at the Buckley house. After all, you claimed Tina was there; she claimed she wasn't. You both gave statements to the police and they contradicted each other. You couldn't both be telling the truth. Miss Murchison had a couple of reasons to care what happened to Ken Buckley. One may have been romantic. The other, if your sources are accurate, may have been legal. He was her client. She might decide to disclose Mr. Buckley's legal business to someone who stood to benefit if he signed the papers. But before she does anything, she wants to know what happened, who killed him, who set the house on fire."

"I wonder," I said, "if Tina's search and Dodie Murchison's business with Ken Buckley are connected."

"They may be. Murchison told you that what troubled him had happened a long time ago. There's no telling what 'a long time ago' means to any person. But if she's in her early thirties, a long time ago may mean when she herself was a teenager, and that could be fifteen years ago."

"I think this is getting more complicated instead of simpler."

"Means you're getting there, honey," Jack said.

Joseph smiled. She seemed amused at how Jack and I interacted. Jack's a pretty low-key guy, and he's helped make me a somewhat more casual person than I was when I left the convent.

"There's another reason Tina may have lied about seeing you at the fire," she said. "Among the possibilities are that she went to see Buckley, and she found him dead and she ran. Or she went to see him and they had their talk, and she left before the murderer arrived. I'm not sure why she was there in that coat if that's what happened, but who knows? Maybe she left him upstairs and went to look for something in the house. Maybe she heard the shot and maybe she didn't. But one possibility is that she saw the murderer, before or after he killed Ken Buckley, and, more important, that he saw her."

"And she got away," I said. "So she had to pretend that she hadn't been there and hadn't seen him to protect her own life."

"It could explain why she lied."

"It also gives us another motive for her being killed, to

keep her quiet. But you know, it doesn't get Dodie Murchison off the hook. She could have killed Tina because Tina killed her lover, and she could have killed Tina because Tina saw her kill Ken."

"I'm sure Murchison knows something that will help you," Joseph said. "I hope you find her before the police do."

"So do I." Jack leaned over and helped Eddie find something that had rolled away. "Chris, would you give Ida Bloom a call? She seemed so sure that there was nothing going on between Ken and Dodie except business. Ask her if she knows what the business was."

Before I had a chance to ask Ida my question, she talked about the funeral yesterday, how many were there, which well-known people showed up, how Eve and her sons had looked. Finally, I asked her about Dodie Murchison.

"You mean the lawyer? The one who came to the house a couple of times?"

"That's the one."

"Eve just said Ken had business with her. I didn't ask and she didn't tell."

"Then Eve knew about it."

"Oh, yes. She mentioned it to me at the beginning of the summer."

I got off as quickly as I could and reported my news.

"So whatever it was, whether it was the prenuptial agreement or something else, he confided in his wife," Joseph said.

"Or lied to her," my cynical husband said.

"I would guess by now Mrs. Buckley could tell a lie from the truth. The fact that she mentioned it to her friend would mean she believed him."

"That leaves the missing diamond earring," I said.

Joseph nodded. "My understanding is that earrings for pierced ears are quite secure. Since it wasn't torn off, we have to assume that it fell off or that someone removed it carefully, either Tina or another person. If it was another person, why take only one? That may be the relevant question."

When Eddie was napping, Joseph and I went outside to stroll and have our last conversation together before she left. We talked mostly about St. Stephen's. They had one novice joining the convent in the fall, and I could tell from Joseph's voice and from her comments that she was worried about the future of the convent. Like so many others, it was aging and little new blood was being added. Joseph was young enough that she had decades ahead of her as an active nun, but there were few of my age and almost none in their twenties. It was depressing to think about, that this wonderful institution might come to an end, especially when the college associated with it had a fine reputation. Already, Joseph had had to hire several secular teachers, one of whom I knew replaced me.

But the nuns who remained were in good health. Sister Cecilia, who was studying nursing in New York, would be returning within a year and she would be able to work in a nearby hospital and care for the elderly nuns in the Villa as well. So ultimately Joseph was upbeat, no surprise to me.

We stopped and chatted with Marti Jorgensen, who was sitting on a chair on the beach in shorts and a shirt. Too cool for a dip today, she told us. But a nice breeze to sit in.

We went back to the house, talking about the Norrises and the Hersheys, what they knew and what they might be holding back.

"What we have to remember," Joseph said, "is that if Tina went around asking questions, she may have stirred up old memories and old grudges, reminded people of buried truths. I think someone may have gotten scared or possibly may have made a connection that went unnoticed for all those years."

"And somehow Ken Buckley was part of it and was made to pay for it."

"Whether he was guilty or not."

Eddie woke up and then it was lunchtime, first his and then ours. And when it was over, Joseph was ready to leave. Jack carried her little bag downstairs and I put it on the wagon, more so that Joseph could see how things happened on Fire Island than because it was too heavy to carry to the ferry.

She had said good-bye to Eddie when he went up for his nap, and now she said it to Jack, and we left.

"There's one last thing," she said, as we approached the bay. In the distance we could see the ferry coming toward the shore, and on the pier were several people with empty red wagons, waiting for friends. "I know Chief La Coste is a dear old man, and he seems like a very kind person and deeply affected by Tina's death, but I don't think he's entirely truthful when he talks about the Great Fire."

"And other things. I'm not sure where that leaves me."

"I'm not sure either, Chris. But I believe the Hersheys and the Norrises are also keeping things to themselves. It looks like the ferry is landing."

"It is. I wish we'd had more time together."

"So do I, but considering that I dashed out on almost no notice at all, it's been a wonderful time."

"For us, too."

We hugged and I carried her bag to the ferry.

The last thing she said was, "Look for that key, Chris, and when you find it, remember what I said."

I waited till the ferry pulled away, waving and throwing kisses, feeling teary at her departure although I was deeply happy she had been able to come. When the moving boat became too small for me to see her anymore, I turned and went back to begin our big cleanup.

22

I walked into the kitchen and found Jack holding up the missing key. "Where did you find it?" I asked incredulously.

"On the hook on the board where it's been the last two weeks."

"And where it wasn't yesterday and today."

"Sister Joseph had it."

"You think so?"

"Pretty sure."

"The last thing she said to me was, 'Look for that key and when you find it, remember what I said.' She took it to make a point."

"What's the point?"

"Let me think a minute." I sat down at the table and closed my eyes, my head in my hand, trying to remember what had been said only yesterday when I discovered it was missing. I had thought Kyle took it. I had asked Marti last night. But Joseph had said something when I saw it was gone. Think, I told myself. "She asked me if I gave it to anyone," I said finally.

"And you said no."

"And it was the truth. I didn't give it to anyone. Someone took it but I didn't give it. You know, the Hersheys had the key to the Norrises' house. They said they didn't give it to anyone."

"But someone who knew where it was usually kept could have taken it. That's opportunity. One of the most basic supports in any proof of a crime is that your suspect had the opportunity to commit it. So technically the Hersheys didn't lie when they said they hadn't given the key to anyone."

"They didn't lie, but they may have withheld the truth. They know who took that key, Jack. They just don't want to say."

When Jack and I were dating, he lived in a small but very nice apartment in Brooklyn Heights. I remember the first time I walked into it, how everything was in place, everything very clean. One never really knows, I guess, whether an apartment is scrubbed in anticipation or out of habit. But Jack turned out to be one of those men who pick up after themselves, and he doesn't leave messes for me to clean up.

So I hadn't been surprised, when I got back to the house, to find he had been vacuuming the living room. I started picking up toys, even flattening myself on the floor to find things under the furniture. Whether or not the murders of Ken Buckley and Tina Frisch were solved, we were going home tomorrow.

We worked hard all afternoon, even after Eddie got up, often working around him. The Jorgensens had invited us for a farewell dinner and we wanted to have the house ready by the time we left. When the phone rang in the middle of the afternoon, I was pretty surprised. I was even more surprised when I answered.

"Is this Chris?" It was a woman.

"Yes, it is."

"This is Dodie Murchison."

"Dodie. I'm glad you called."

"I need to talk to you. Can you meet me tonight?"

"Where?"

"Well, not on Fire Island. I'm not setting foot on that island till this is cleared up."

"Tonight would be very difficult with the reduced ferry schedule. But we're leaving tomorrow after lunch."

There was silence. Then, "I guess one day won't make that much difference. Is it true that Tina was murdered?"

"It's true. It happened Wednesday night. Her body was discovered Thursday morning." Those were facts she could find out from anyone in Blue Harbor and probably from the newspaper as well.

"That's what I thought. Where do you live?"

"On the north side of the Long Island Sound."

"OK. I can get there. I'd rather not meet you in your home. Is there someplace—?"

"Yes. There's a residence for retarded adults in my town, Oakwood. My cousin lives there. What time do you want to meet?"

"You call it. You have a family. Pick a time that's convenient."

"Seven."

"Seven is good. How do I get there?"

"It's called Greenwillow," I said, and I gave her directions as though she were coming from New York.

"I'm trusting you, Chris. If you bring the police with you—"

"I won't. I'll come alone. We can sit in the administrator's office and talk. You won't have to give your name when you come in. Just say you're looking for me. I'll get there early."

"I appreciate this. You won't let the police know, any police."

"I won't let anyone know."

"See you tomorrow at seven."

We stopped our cleaning long enough to discuss this

new turn of events. Jack didn't look particularly happy. "She's a suspect in a homicide," he said, as though I needed reminding.

"She has information that we need. I don't think she's going to take me hostage in Greenwillow."

"Maybe not, but neither of us is convinced she's innocent."

"Or the opposite. I have to do this, Jack. She knows things that we don't know. If I tell Curt Springer where she'll be tomorrow night, he'll have her arrested. She's an attorney and that could be the end of her career."

"She's an attorney, you're right, and she probably knows how to lie very artfully."

"Artfully," I said. "That doesn't sound like the kind of word you'd use."

He grinned. "OK, have it your way. Suppose we ask Elsie Rivers to come and stay with Eddie, and I'll sit in another room just to prove to myself that I'm wasting my time."

"She said not to tell any police she was coming."

"You already told me. I'm police."

"I hadn't thought of it that way. OK, I'll call Elsie. She's probably dying to see Eddie anyway."

So that's what we did. Elsie is an old friend of my mother's, and she's as much a surrogate grandmother as Eddie will ever have. She was his first baby-sitter and she was born to the job.

From that moment on, I flew through my work.

Everything was a "last" after we finished. We dashed to the pool and took our last swims. We walked on the beach and told Eddie we were going home tomorrow. We said good-bye to the few people we recognized as we walked. We went back to the house and packed away everything that was dry and hung up the suits we had just worn on the line out back. We picked the blueberries that were left on the bushes and brought them inside. Eddie's little fingers popped one after the other into his mouth. This fall we would buy a couple of bushes and plant them in our backyard.

We got to the Jorgensens' after Eddie was fast asleep and set him down in their bedroom as we had done before. Then we joined Al and Marti on the deck for cocktails.

"Find that key?" Al asked, as he handed me a glass.

"We did. It was just misplaced."

"Nothing causes more panic than a missing key," Marti said, and she told us a tale of a calamitous situation she had lived through a couple of years ago.

"Nice woman, that Sister Joseph," Al said afterwards.

"Thank you. She's a good friend and whenever I introduce her, people are impressed."

"We didn't realize you'd been a nun yourself."

I did some explaining, having become used to the surprise of people who see me as a wife and mother, as a teacher, as a volunteer. When I'd dispensed with that, Al said, "Well, I don't know if you've heard the news, but Curt Springer thinks he has a suspect in the murders."

I looked at Jack, who said, "The lawyer?"

"Right you are. He's got her fingerprints all over the area where Tina's body was found, and some other things that he isn't talking about. Murchison, I think her name is. You know she got out on the first ferry the next morning."

"I heard. I'd sure like to find out what other evidence he has. And how does he tie her in to the Buckley murder?"

"Says her prints were picked up in the Buckley house, too. That's pretty amazing if she wasn't there."

"Has he found her yet?" I asked.

"Not when I talked to him. They've got one of those APBs out on her in several states. They'll find her. You don't often find a woman committing a murder by strangling, do you? But she probably does a lot of exercising. All those young people do."

Marti threw her hands up. "Al really thinks that woman did it. I don't. I could believe a woman would shoot Ken Buckley. To tell the truth, I'm surprised none of them did it before now." She laughed. "But putting your hands around the neck of a young girl? I couldn't do it, not if she'd just killed my child. It's too, you know, personal. I'd go for the gun."

"You and Al didn't see anything that night, did you?" Jack asked.

"Not a thing. We always sit facing out back. We paid for that view and we get our money's worth." From the back of their house they could see the ocean past the Margulies's backyard.

We talked and ate and had a good time, and finally we said good-bye. Marti kissed our sleeping son and we all wished each other a good winter.

"And no strong winds," Al said. It was the Fire Island homeowner's dearest wish.

When we were ready to leave the next day, Jack looked around for Chief Springer but didn't find him at any of his haunts. We had dismissed the discovery of Dodie's fingerprints in the Buckley house as meaningless. We knew she had been there so it wasn't surprising that she had touched things. Jack even speculated that Springer had nothing else in the way of evidence and was just grandstanding.

After Eddie was sleeping, we walked down to the ferry, pulling the red wagon with our luggage, hoping Eddie would get his nap as we moved from island to ferry to car and then to the long drive home. We hung up the empty wagon on its hook and locked it safely just before the ferry pulled alongside the dock.

All the way home we talked about Harry Hershey. He had been a fireman and knew Ken Buckley. Maybe they had an agreement. When the Norrises weren't home, Ken could take their key from the Hersheys' house and use the empty house next door for whatever he wanted. But something terrible and unforeseen happened and the house burned down. Now, fifteen years later, Ken decided to make amends in a way that would implicate the Hersheys and Harry took revenge. It was a new look at a case that was baffling me more each day.

It was the longest we had ever left our house empty and as we entered, we both immediately felt the need of fresh air. Jack went around opening windows and turning on fans and pretty soon we were breathing easier. Eddie seemed to recognize the house and especially his bedroom, and he sat on the floor and looked at toys he had forgotten he had.

"You're home now, Eddie," I said.

He uttered a few syllables and crawled over to his crib, grabbed the highest part he could reach, and pulled himself up to a standing position.

"Jack," I shouted down the stairs. "Come up here. Eddie's standing!" I could hardly believe it. It had happened so suddenly.

Hanging on with both hands, Eddie turned to me and gave me a big smile.

"You know you've done something wonderful, don't you?" I said.

Jack bounded up the stairs and into the room. "How do you like that?" He edged closer to the crib, as though he might upset the little applecart.

Eddie looked at him and giggled. Then he let go one hand, lost his grip and his footing, and dropped onto his rump, bursting into tears as he hit the floor.

I picked him up and told him how wonderful he was, and he put his head on my shoulder and whimpered a little. Then we began to get ready for bath and supper.

There were a million phone messages, none of them very significant. When I had a free moment, I called Melanie Gross back, since she was the person I missed most.

"Chris! You're back. What on earth is going on out there on Fire Island?"

"Did you hear something?"

"Uncle Max got a call from a fireman that the chief had been murdered. What happened?"

I gave her the condensed version and promised to get together with her the next afternoon. She had already begun teaching, as I would in a couple of days myself. Home barely an hour, we felt that the summer seemed a long time ago.

We had stopped at the Oakwood Deli and gotten cold cuts for our dinner and the makings of tomorrow's breakfast since the house was as bare as we had left it. When Eddie was asleep in his own crib, we sat down to wolf down the sandwiches. Elsie came while we were still eating, and Jack took off in his car to get to Greenwillow first. It was only a few minutes' drive from home, and I had arranged tonight's meeting yesterday by telephone, so I got Elsie comfortable and then dashed out myself.

My car is so old and has so much mileage on it that it's become a bone of contention between Jack and me. He uses his car in his police work. As a detective, he needs to drive to crime scenes and he usually uses his own car, so it has to be in top-notch condition. My car takes me where I need to go, gives me very little trouble, and makes Jack very unhappy. He imagines breakdowns when I am alone or with Eddie. He fears complications that will endanger us. He wants me to buy a new car that he can count on, that will be more comfortable, that will protect us from a hostile world. I want to keep this car until it passes peacefully into oblivion and then, and only then, will I think about its replacement.

On this September evening, I got into it with a quick prayer that it would start after two weeks of sitting in the garage. The battery sounded weak as I turned the key, and nothing happened on the first try. I knew that in case of real trouble, Elsie would let me take hers, but I was determined. I took a deep breath, turned the key again, and after a fearful moment, the motor caught, roaring into life. I said, "Thank you, sweetheart," aloud, backed out of the garage, and was on my way.

23

Greenwillow has a small parking lot on its premises for the parents and other relatives of the residents who come to visit, usually on the weekends. As I turned into the drive, I saw that Jack's car was not there, but I assumed he had dropped it somewhere, perhaps in the nearby bank parking lot, and walked the rest of the way.

I went to the front door and rang the bell. Jonesy, one of the permanent staff, opened the door and welcomed me.

"Your husband's here," she said. "He said I'm not to say anything to the woman you're meeting."

"That's right. She isn't here, then?"

"Not yet. Would you like to go into the office?"

"Sure." I went in, leaving the door open. "If the doorbell rings, I'll answer it, OK?"

"That's fine. I'll be around if you need me."

I sat down to wait. This was Virginia McAlpine's office, and she had moved all the furniture and books from the old Greenwillow in a nearby town to this wonderful new location right in Oakwood, a large, old house that had been converted into a comfortable residence where my cousin Gene lived. It appeared that Virginia had been able to duplicate her old office. I got up and looked at the books in the large bookcases built into the wall. As I was reading titles, the doorbell rang.

I went to the front door, unlocked it, and pulled it open. Dodie Murchison, a silk scarf around her head and tinted glasses on her face, stood there. "I found it," she said, and walked inside.

I asked her if she wanted any coffee or juice but she didn't. She just wanted to get into a room with a door that closed, sit down, and begin talking.

"Have you learned anything?" she asked first, pulling the scarf off and shaking her hair.

"A few things, but I'm no closer to determining who murdered Ken Buckley or Tina Frisch than I was several days ago."

"I wish I could pull a name out of a hat for you but I can't. But I know several things that you may not, and perhaps they'll help you. And I'll work with you in any way I can to get this settled. I know the Blue Harbor chief thinks I committed these acts, but I didn't, Chris. And the sooner we find the person or persons who did, the sooner I can go back to living my life."

"Why don't you tell me what you know?" I suggested. I had my pen and notebook and was sitting in a leather chair.

"I have to be sure you aren't recording this," she said. She looked around the room, then walked to the book-case and surveyed the shelves, pulling an occasional book out. She then went to the desk and checked the drawers, all of which were apparently locked. She moved things in the room, looked behind and under furniture, then turned to me. "I'm sorry, Chris. I need to check your person."

I stood and raised my arms as though I were a victim in a Western. She came and patted me down gently, and, I thought, with embarrassment and misgivings.

"OK. Let's begin." She sat in the other leather chair, positioned so we could look at each other. "I met Ken

Buckley in New York, not on the beach at Fire Island as you surmised. The circumstances don't matter. What's relevant is that he had been carrying a load of guilt for a number of years and he wanted to alleviate it the only way he knew how, by giving someone money. It goes back a lot of years, to another Labor Day, in fact. when he got a phone call that someone needed help.

"He wasn't the fire chief at that time but on that day he was filling in for the fire chief, and for the police chief that preceded Curtis Springer as well, and that may be why he received the call. He was very careful when he was talking to me not to mention names of people who might be incriminated by his story. So you'll understand if I speak of people without identifying them."

I had no way of knowing whether this was true or whether she knew the names and had simply decided to keep them to herself, but it didn't matter. If her story pointed in the direction Joseph, Jack, and I had been heading, I would recognize many of the players. "That's fine," I said.

"The call came at night from a house in Blue Harbor. He went there and found that a young girl. a teenager, I believe, was crying hysterically. The story he was told was that she had picked up—or met—a man on the beach that afternoon, a young man, probably in his twenties, and they had spent the afternoon together. Before they realized it, it was evening and the last ferry had left for Bay Shore. She didn't want to tell her parents about him, but she knew of an empty house—neighbors of her parents owned it and they had left the island—so she told him he could stay there if he was careful and didn't leave any traces that he'd been there. What happened was that when she was showing him the house, he attacked her and tried to rape her." She stopped, her feelings plainly shown on her face.

"What did she do?" I asked, certain now of what the answer would be, an important missing piece in my puzzle.

"She stabbed him with a kitchen knife and killed him."

Even expecting it, I felt a chill. "And then she had a problem."

"Then she had a big problem. She didn't know what to do and she was afraid to tell anyone, especially her parents. But eventually she did. They discussed the alternatives, one of which was that they would leave the body in the empty house for the owners to discover when they came out to Fire Island the next time. They discarded that plan, and decided to get help from someone they thought they could trust, and that someone turned out to be Ken Buckley." She stopped for a moment and then said, "You know, I could use a cup of coffee after all, if you know how to get hold of some."

"Sure." I left the office and found Jonesy. We went to the kitchen together and I saw a carafe half-full. Jonesy put it all into a thermos pitcher and we carried that and a couple of mugs back to Virginia's office. I didn't let Jonesy in, so Dodie could keep her privacy.

Dodie was walking around the room nervously, as though still looking for a recording device, but when the coffee arrived, she seemed to relax a little. We sat and sipped for a while and finally she smiled.

"That's better. I didn't know how much I needed that."

"Take your time."

"Well, not too long. I have to get back to—" She didn't finish. Her whereabouts were not my business.

"I understand. You were saying that they decided not to leave the body for the owners of the house to find, and instead they called Ken Buckley to help."

"That's what happened. Ken went over. He knew the people, knew the girl—Ken knew everyone. He assessed the situation as I've described it to you. The man was dead, there was no question about that. By the time Ken arrived, he had probably been dead for some time, possibly as long as an hour or so. They talked. Ken told me how very deeply he felt for the girl's situation. He believed her story that the man had tried to rape her, that she had grabbed a kitchen knife and stabbed him with it and that the wound had been fatal. He told me he could think of no other reason for the girl to have done what she did, and he may also have said that the victim's clothes indicated he might have been starting to undress. And he said eventually it came down to the question of what to do with the body. He didn't want the girl involved in a homicide."

"Did he know who the victim was?"

"He took all the ID he could find and kept it. The man's name was William Jamieson. There was an address, keys, but no documents for a car. He had told the girl he didn't have one, that he had hitched a ride with some guys and told them not to wait if he didn't make the last ferry. He had apparently come out to see a girl he'd met somewhere else, but he never found her. He thought maybe he'd taken the wrong ferry and ended up in the wrong town on Fire Island."

"So whoever she was, she thought she was stood up and it wasn't a serious enough relationship for her to follow up on it."

"That's the way it sounded to me."

"What did they do with the body?"

"He burned it. It wasn't as simple as that, of course. Nothing ever is. The house had a fairly new country-pine floor and it was covered with blood in the kitchen where Jamieson had been stabbed. The blood had seeped into the wood, and there was no way they could clean up the floor and get rid of the stain so that the owners would not know something had happened there. So Ken decided that the house would burn down.

"He gave me some of the details but they really don't matter. He was both acting fire chief and acting police chief that day, and the fire was in his domain so it gave him the right to issue orders. He arranged things so that the body would burn and he allowed no one to go inside except himself and one other person until the next day."

"The father of the girl," I said. "He used to be a volunteer fireman."

She looked at me with surprise. "You know all this."

"I knew about the fire. I didn't know there was a homicide, but of course, that answers a lot of questions. I spoke to people who I assume were the parents of the girl. There are pictures in their living room of a daughter at her wedding and later with her husband and children."

"I see." She refilled her mug and sipped, leaning back in the comfortable chair. She looked as though the last few days had taken a toll on her. Her face seemed thinner. "How did you come to them?"

"I believed the murder of Ken Buckley and the torching of his house were retaliation for some past act. But everyone seemed to like him, even though it was quite well known that he was a philanderer. Of course, someone I talked to may well have been putting on an act, but I still don't know who that was. Every time I start to suspect someone, something comes up to exclude that person. It was the fire at the Buckley house that made me think the Great Fire of fifteen years ago might be connected. The bullet in Ken's head killed him, not the fire. Someone set the house on fire to make a point, not to kill him."

"So your questions led you to what you call the Great Fire."

"That's right. But I don't want to stop you. You have more to tell me."

"Yes, I do. There's not much more about the accidental killing and the fire. The house, I gather, was a total loss. The owners were led to believe that they'd left something on the stove when they left the house, that whatever it was caught fire, and that was that. Ken said they moved to another town on Fire Island. They sold the property and the new people rebuilt. But that has nothing to do with the story.

"The rest of the story is a tale of guilt. Whatever you may think of Ken Buckley, he had a conscience and his conscience told him that whoever this William Jamieson was, he must have had a family. He decided to try to find any relatives of Jamieson's that might still be living and give them an anonymous gift or, if that proved too difficult, to leave something to them in his will. As an estate attorney, I often have to find missing heirs, and I agreed to try to find Jamieson's family. We had several documents to work from, a Social Security card, a driver's license, a few very old snapshots, and a couple of other things. They led me to a dead end. The Social Security card was for a deceased person with the same name. I think the name was assumed at some point in his life, and I don't have a clue what his real name was. Ken authorized me to keep at it. He felt that somewhere out there"—she waved her right hand—"were people who had been waiting all these years for the person known as William Jamieson to return."

"There were," I said. "Tina Frisch was one of them."

"Tina Frisch? Tina Frisch knew William Jamieson?" It was clear the news had surprised her.

"She thought he was someone known to her family. She'd been looking into his disappearance all summer."

"I was unaware of that. What happened to her is a terrible story, a tragic story. Someone killed her after I spoke to her Wednesday night."

"Do you know who?"

"I don't have any idea. But I'm sure Tina knew him."

"How do you know that?"

"She told me she knew who killed Ken Buckley, not who it was, but that she knew who it was."

"Why did you go to see her, Dodie?"

"Because of what you said, that she had been at the Buckley fire, that she was trying to hide her face as she left, that she denied having been there. I'd been working all summer on trying to trace William Jamieson for Ken Buckley and suddenly this fire happens, Ken is murdered—it was getting too close to home. I figured it would be safe to talk to her because she wasn't likely to have a weapon, especially if she was wearing shorts like the rest of us. I walked over to the house where she was a grouper. She came downstairs and we went out for a walk. She was pretty tense. At first she didn't want to say anything. Then she asked me if she could be my client and I said, 'Sure. Give me a dollar and I'm your attorney.' She didn't have any money on her so she unscrewed a small diamond earring she was wearing and handed it to me. She said she'd buy it back later."

"The missing earring," I breathed.

Dodie gave me a wry smile. "I'll bet that gave the crime scene unit something to worry about."

"All of us. It hadn't been forcibly removed and it never turned up in the house."

"Well, I have it. At some point I'll turn it over to the proper authorities."

"You said Tina knew her killer."

"Tina had an appointment with Ken Buckley during the Labor Day picnic. She wasn't clear what she went to see him about, but she told me she found him dead in his bed. On her way out, she saw the person she believed killed him."

"But she didn't name him."

"No. It was someone she knew in Blue Harbor. She looked around as she was telling me this, as though he might be there, as though he might hear."

A chill went through me. Harry Hershey lived a five-minute walk from the Kleins' house. Al Jorgensen lived near the Kleins' house. Kyle lived in the Kleins' house. But Kyle had given me the notebook that Danielle had found in the refrigerator. Would he have done that if he had killed Tina? I rubbed my forehead. The notebook had told us very little besides confirming what we already knew. He could have taken a calculated risk. But I couldn't believe it was Kyle. He seemed so real and earnest; he had liked Tina.

But Ken might have told Harry Hershey he was look-ing for Jamieson's family, and Harry might have feared his daughter would face charges if the true events of that Labor Day night became public. He might have walked over to the Buckley house on Monday. . . .

"Something wrong?"

"I'm just trying to think who it might be, and it's very distressing."

"It's distressing to know I'm a suspect in her murder."

"I know."

"I told her to go to the police with what she knew and she said she would do that as soon as she left Fire Island. She was obviously very uncomfortable being there. I ad-vised her to leave the island as soon as possible, which was the next day. And I decided that would be the best thing for me to do, too. I didn't like the idea of a killer walking around. someone who might be my next-door neighbor. So after I left her, I went back to my house and packed my bags."

"Dodie, your fingerprints were found all over the grip on Tina's handlebars and I think also on the gate to the crawl space."

She thought about it. "She said she wanted to go somewhere, to say good-bye to someone. She needed the bike. I walked her back to her house—we were still talking—and we went for the bike. There were a couple in there, I think, and she had trouble pulling out the one she wanted. I helped her. That's all. When you touch something, you leave prints. I left mine."

"I thought as much."

"How do they know they're my prints? I've never been printed that I can recall."

"The crime scene unit went over the house you'd been living in and matched prints in the house with prints on the bike. It's not a certainty but it's pretty close."

"Too damn close."

"Tina didn't tell you what her interest in Ken Buckley was?"

"Not really."

"She was looking into the elusive Mr. William Jamieson."

"So it's all tied together."

"Yes."

"What was her connection?" Dodie asked.

"She called him Uncle Bill, but she thought he might be her natural father. He was a friend of her mother's. He visited a lot."

"Amazing. She probably would have told me the next time we met. We made an appointment for tomorrow in my office. And I was going to give her her earring back." As she spoke, she opened her handbag, a large, elegant, black bag, and pulled out a tissue. When she opened it, a small glittering stone lay in her hand. "A dollar's worth of diamond," she said.

24

We talked a little while longer. She was interested in how I had learned as much as I had and I told her a lot of it, but kept a number of things to myself, as I was sure she had also. Finally I asked her the question I most wanted the answer to.

"What did Ken Buckley do with William Jamieson's body?"

"He wouldn't tell me. He said he disposed of it and that he didn't want to say any more about it. I know, because I found out, that there's a body bag kept at the firehouse, just in case it's ever needed. So it's possible he used that. But I have no idea what he did with the body. And there are things I'd rather not know, if you know what I mean."

I nodded. We had been talking for quite a while and it had been a long day. I felt that I trusted her, but not completely. She had good answers to my questions, but she'd had time to prepare for them. "Are you going to turn yourself in?" I asked finally.

"I haven't decided. I have to think about my career. I am totally innocent with respect to these homicides, but I have information that the police may need. I'm fairly sure I was the last person to see Tina alive, except for the person who killed her. I can't withhold that information very long. I'd appreciate it if you'd tell me if you have any viable suspects."

"They come and go in my head, Dodie. It could be the father of the girl who was almost raped. Ken helped him out of the tightest spot he'd ever been in and he must be very grateful for that, but if Ken told him he was looking for the family of William Jamieson, the father may have feared his daughter's role in Jamieson's death would be exposed."

"That might happen inadvertently. Good point."

"And I think about the groupers in Tina's house, but they don't have any motive that I can think of. If we can figure out who William Jamieson really was, maybe we could go on from there. This is the first I've heard that there was a homicide in that house fifteen years ago, and also the first I've heard that Tina's supposed Uncle Bill was living under an assumed name."

"And this is the first that I knew there was a connection between Tina and William Jamieson," Dodie said, as though to thank me in return for the information I had given her. "So we've both learned something tonight, and unless you have a better idea, I think the next step has to be to talk to Tina's mother."

"I agree. She ought to remember Jamieson and maybe she knows the truth about him."

Dodie reached into the still-open pocketbook. "I have her address." She pulled out a notepad covered in burgundy leather and turned a couple of small pages. Then she wrote on a clean page, tore it out, and handed it to me. "I gather the mother has had a few husbands. That's her current name."

She had written "Sally Holland" and an address in New Jersey. "Have you called her?" I asked.

"No. I didn't see any reason to. Tina hadn't told me about looking for Jamieson. She was a little mysterious

about what she was going to see Ken Buckley about. I
thought, maybe—"

"I understand."

"Are you up to this? Talking to the Holland woman?"

I had been trying to calculate whether to take Eddie
with me or go by myself. But either way, someone had to
talk to Tina's mother. "I'll go."

"How soon?"

"I'll try tomorrow. I teach on Tuesday and I can't miss
the first class of the semester."

"I'll call you tomorrow night then." She closed her bag.

"Tell me one thing," I said. "Why did you come to
me? Why did you tell me all this?"

"I trusted you. You didn't appear to have an ulterior
motive. I was sure you hadn't killed anyone, and you
seemed to have uncovered some interesting tidbits. When
I talked to Tina that last night, it was clear she had lied to
the police and you had told the truth. And maybe—I
don't know—maybe I just didn't know where else to
turn."

"I'll do my best. I know how important this is to you."

She stood and put her scarf back on, covering her
beautiful hair except for a little on her forehead. Then she
put the tinted glasses back on although it was already
dark out.

"When did you hear about Tina's murder?" I asked.

"When I was nearly home." She stopped, as if trying
to recall. "I took the first ferry to Bay Shore that morning. I hadn't eaten anything so I stopped somewhere—I
can't even remember where—and had a big breakfast. I
made some notes, the names of lawyers I know who
might be able to handle this better than I. I was there for
quite a while. Before I got on the highway, I stopped again
at a farmers' market and bought some fresh fruits and
vegetables."

"So it took you a long time to get home."

"Much longer than usual. I had the radio on in the car and before I got to my apartment, they mentioned it. All I could think of was that everyone in that house knew I'd been to see Tina the night before, and the last I'd seen her she was off on her bicycle. I had no idea where she'd been killed or how. But someone was bound to make a connection between us. I decided not to go home."

I opened the door of the office and looked out. From time to time during our talk I had heard sounds, mostly laughter, from another room. It was Sunday night and I assumed the residents were watching a movie in the game room. No one was around. I walked Dodie to the front door and we shook hands. The last I saw of her, her silk scarf was blowing in the breeze.

"The picture is certainly filling in," Jack said. We had come home in two separate cars, chatted with Elsie for a while, and now we were sipping coffee in the family room with Eddie safely upstairs in his crib.

"And Ken Buckley turns out to be a man of conscience. I think his wife must have known all about this, don't you?"

"It's likely. If he told her he was talking to Murchison about diverting some funds to Jamieson's heirs, she probably knows what happened that night."

"And the Hersheys have to know. They're the ones who called Ken in the first place."

"It was to everyone's advantage to keep the secret. There's no statute of limitations on murder, and there's been no investigation to determine whether the death of Jamieson was murder or self-defense or any one of a whole lot of other possible charges. Everyone involved is potentially liable as co-conspirators, actual suspects, or material witnesses."

"Poor Mrs. Norris. She was so sure she hadn't left anything on that stove. But she had to accept what the fire department's investigation turned up."

"Phony investigation," Jack corrected me. "They started with the result, not with the search, and worked back from there."

I looked at my watch. "I guess I'd better get this over with. I have to call and see if Tina's mother is home and if I can come over tomorrow."

"Good luck."

I dialed, half hoping she wouldn't answer. Talking to the mother of a murdered child filled me with dread. But she answered the phone and I told her my name and plunged into my mission.

"I knew your daughter, Mrs. Holland," I said. "She was staying at a house across the street from ours on Fire Island. I just came home today."

"You were there?" She sounded surprised. "You were there when she—when Tina died?"

"Yes, I was. I wonder if I could drive out and talk to you tomorrow. Will you be home?"

"I can be home, sure. When do you want to come?"

"It'll take me a couple of hours. About eleven?"

"I'll be there."

I let my breath out as I got off the phone. I had forgotten to ask whether Tina had been buried yet, but surely the funeral couldn't be tomorrow or she wouldn't have made the appointment.

"All set?" Jack asked.

"Yes. I'll just call Elsie and let her know it'll be a long day."

25

Jack works the ten-to-six in the detective squad at the Sixty-fifth Precinct in Brooklyn. It gives us a chance to have breakfast together, for him to see Eddie for a while before he leaves. Monday through Thursday he goes to evening law school, and that Monday was the day the fall semester began. He had taken care of registration and books before we left for Fire Island, so he was all set when he kissed us good-bye.

I was feeling a little sad to see him go. We had had two wonderful weeks together, and three months of having him home at a normal hour. I would miss his company at dinner, not to mention his cooking, and all those little times during the day when we had enjoyed being in the same room at the same time. There was something very final about the first day of work after Labor Day, the first day of school, the first time you put your headlights on to come home at night.

But I had a place to go and I got moving fast, leaving a telephone message for Melanie that I might not be back in time to see her but I would if I could. Then I scooped up Eddie and the bag that always went with him, and drove to Elsie's house.

It was a long drive just to get to the George Washington Bridge, which crosses the Hudson River into New

Jersey. Then it was another long drive to Sally Holland's town just outside of New Brunswick. I missed my intended eleven o'clock arrival and needed directions when I got off the New Jersey Turnpike, but I found her house at last. It was a small, one-story house on a street of similar houses. A cousin of hers opened the door and showed me into the family room where Sally Holland was sitting and watching television. When we'd introduced ourselves and I had expressed my sympathy, she turned off the set.

She was a thin woman in her forties with the same coloring as her daughter. She looked sad and drab. She was wearing a pair of gray slacks and a black cotton sweater and only some bright red lipstick gave her any color.

"Mrs. Holland," I began, "do you know why Tina went to Fire Island this summer?"

"To have fun. Why does anyone go?"

"Most people go for that reason. Tina went to track down someone she'd known in her childhood." I watched her eyes. First they looked distant; then they brightened.

"Who would that be?" she asked carefully.

"Someone she thought of as Uncle Bill."

"Billy," the woman whispered. "She was looking for Billy."

"I believe his name was William Jamieson."

"Yeah, that's who he was, Bill Jamieson. She never forgot him."

"She thought he might be her father."

Sally Holland shook her head. "Bill wasn't her father. He was a friend. I met him in a funny way and we got to be friends. I was good to him and he was good to us. Up to a point."

"Did you know him long?"

"Oh, yeah. Years."

"Was he a boyfriend?"

"At the beginning, maybe. Then it cooled off. He'd go away and come back. If he needed a place to stay for a while, I'd give him a bed to sleep in."

"What kind of person was he?" I asked. "Was he ever violent?"

"He could slap you around a little. What man doesn't?" She smiled as though we were sharing a secret. It made me feel very uneasy. "But he could be nice, too. And he liked Tina. He used to bring her things, toys, a hat from Texas once. I think he even got her a new bike."

"You knew he was going to Fire Island that last time you saw him, didn't you?"

"He told me he was going. Said he'd met a girl somewheres, she was going to be there. They couldn't go together for some reason. I think she lived in one place and he lived somewhere else. So he got a ride or took the train. The Long Island Railroad, maybe?"

"I think that goes out there."

"Then you take a boat, right?"

"Yes."

"Sounded nice to me. It was all beaches and ocean. You could spend the day on the beach and maybe have a picnic."

"Do you remember what day he went out?"

"How could I remember after such a long time? It was a holiday, I think. The Fourth of July, maybe." She thought about it. "Maybe it was Labor Day."

"And then what happened?"

"That was it. Nothing happened. I never saw him again."

"Did you try calling him?"

"There was nowhere to call. Sometimes he stayed with me, sometimes he stayed with a friend. He probably stayed with girlfriends, too, when that worked out."

"I guess Tina must've been upset."

"Oh, yeah. She wanted her Uncle Billy something awful. But I told her, 'He's gone, honey. Let's hope he's happy wherever he is.'" She stopped and looked as if something had just clicked. "You know where he is?"

"Not exactly, but I may know why you never heard from him again."

"He's dead, isn't he?" She squeezed her hands together and her face looked bleak. "I knew it. I knew it years ago. He would've called. He would've dropped in, 'specially if he needed something. Like I said, I was good to him."

"I think he's dead, Mrs. Holland. I don't know for sure but I—"

"He's dead. I know it." She patted her chest to show me where she knew it best.

"You must have told Tina where he went on that last trip."

"I could've. I don't remember. Maybe I said it a while ago. I can't even remember where he went, except that it was Fire Island."

"She was trying to find out what happened to him. She wrote in a notebook that she thought Bill was her father."

"He wasn't."

"I understand, but that's what she thought. She wanted to know what happened to him. She asked around to see if there were any drownings that summer or if anyone got hurt in a fight."

"Is that why she was killed? Because she was looking for Bill?"

"I think it's connected. I'm not sure exactly how. I found something out, just last night. I learned that William Jamieson wasn't his real name."

"So that's it," she said, as though something had just made sense after a long time. "He said to me once—I met someone named Jamieson and I asked Bill if he could be related, and he said he wasn't related to anyone named Jamieson, and I said, 'How can that be? You've got a dad and you've got brothers and sisters. You gotta have relatives with that name.' But he said he didn't, and I could tell he didn't want to talk about it. So I let it alone."

"Do you have any idea what his real name was?"

"He never said a word. He never even said Bill wasn't his real name."

"If we knew his real name," I said carefully, "it might give us a clue to who killed Tina."

"How's that?" she said.

"Tina was asking questions and poking around all summer. It's kind of complicated, but her death may be connected with another murder a few days earlier, and both of them may be connected to Bill's death fifteen years ago."

"Fifteen years ago. Is it that long already?"

"Yes. If we could just find out who Bill really was, where he came from, who his family is, maybe we could find some answers."

She was silent for a minute. She folded and refolded her hands. "He left some things here. I gave away the clothes a long time ago because I figured if he came back, they wouldn't fit him anymore anyway, but there's a couple of other things if I can just find them. You want to take a look?"

"I'd like to."

She got up and I followed her to a door in the kitchen that led to the basement. We went downstairs and she walked over to an assortment of cartons and suitcases that filled a corner. I couldn't imagine how she could find anything, but it turned out that many of the boxes were labeled and after a few minutes, she pulled one out.

"Maybe in here," she said, "but I can't promise."

We opened it and she fished around inside. The first

thing she pulled out was a pair of small pink satin ballet slippers, tied together. She held them and looked at them, and tears rolled down her cheeks. "I wanted her to be a dancer," she said. "She was so delicate and beautiful."

"Maybe this isn't the time," I said softly.

"If I don't do it now, I'll never do it." She set the slippers aside and went back to her rummaging. "Here's something." She pulled an old brown envelope out and handed it to me. "These are papers I found after he left. Take a look. Maybe something's inside with his real name on it."

The envelope was about nine by twelve, and inside was an assortment of papers, including minuscule want ad clippings from a newspaper. Whether he had applied for the jobs or just thought about it, I couldn't tell. They weren't marked in any way. There was a small snapshot of himself with Tina and Sally, possibly in this very backyard. He was a good-looking, dark-haired young man with strong arms and shoulders. I handed it to her and she said, "Oh, look at that," and held it a little distance from her face, as though she were becoming farsighted and needed her glasses.

It was the only picture in the envelope, but there were a couple of letters, all addressed to William Jamieson at this address, that looked like form rejections for jobs. There was an empty key ring with a plastic bottle of beer hanging from it, and at the bottom I found a small penknife with a ring at one end so you could hang it from a chain or key ring. Engraved on it was the name "Buzzy." I showed it to her.

"I never saw that before." She took it in her hand, looked at it, opened it and closed it.

"Everything seems to be addressed to William Jamieson," I said. Just to make sure I hadn't missed anything, I spilled everything in the envelope out onto the top of a

closed carton. A folded yellow sheet of lined paper was
hidden between two of the typewritten letters. I unfolded
it and spread it out. It was handwritten in pencil, a letter
that began, "Dear Buzzy."

"This is something," I said. "Listen.

> 'Dear Buzzy,
>   Hope things are working out for you. It's a cold win-
> ter here and the snows pretty hi. Did you get that job at
> the warehouse? That kind of work pays pretty good
> and its a good place to get started. Maybe you'l get to
> be president of the compny some day. Ha, ha. Give us
> a call. Mother misses you a lot. Me too.
>   Your loving Dad' "

"So his real name was Buzzy?"

"Probably his nickname. It's not going to help very
much. May I take this with me? I promise I'll get it
back to you."

"Sure, take it. What'm I gonna do with it? Put it back
in the box?"

I refolded it and we went back upstairs. I didn't see anything further that I could do here. I hadn't learned much
and had made her more upset than she'd been when I
walked in the house. "Have you had the funeral yet?" I
asked.

"It was Saturday. They didn't keep her long, and I didn't
want to wait till today. So it's over."

"Thank you for helping out. If I learn anything, I'll let
you know." I wrote down my name and address, as I
always did, and gave it to her.

"You came a long way," she said.

"I want to find out who killed Tina."

"You know he took one of her earrings?" She sounded
very angry.

"I heard. You may get that back."

"I'd like to. She loved those earrings. They were real diamonds. My husband gave them to her when she turned twenty-one."

"If it turns up, I'm sure they'll return it to you."

I picked up my bag and put the yellow letter in it. Then we walked to the front door.

"I don't know if I should tell you this," Sally Holland said. "It's about Bill. He only told me because we were friends and he trusted me."

I looked at her, wondering what she had to say.

"The day I met him—he told me this a long time later—I picked him up at a bus stop. I never did anything like that before but I was in a good mood about something, and he was standing there with this little bag and he didn't look dangerous or anything, so I stopped the car and asked him if I could give him a lift." She kind of smiled and for a moment her face lost its forlornness. "It was a lucky day for both of us. He told me afterwards he'd just gotten out of prison."

"He was in prison? Here in New Jersey?"

"Yeah. Trenton State. That's south of here. They let him out that morning and he hitchhiked from there. It was just our luck that I was driving by."

"Did he tell you what he was in for?"

"It was nothing, pilfering or something. You know, shoplifting." She made it sound very mild, very offhand, as though everybody did it but poor Billy had gotten caught.

"Mrs. Holland, do you remember the date?"

"Oh yeah. It was Tina's birthday, September twenty-second."

"And the year? If we know the day and the year, we may be able to find out who he was."

"Let me think a minute." She went into the kitchen and

came back with a piece of paper with numbers written on it in pencil. She handed it to me. "I could be off by a year, but try this. I think Tina was five that day."

"So you knew him for a few years."

"A few years. That was it."

"Thanks for telling me. I'll keep you posted, and if you remember anything else or find anything with his name on it, please let me know."

"And the earring," she said.

"I'll do my best."

26

It turned out I hadn't been there very long. I found a place to stop and eat lunch, and then I got back in the car and just drove without stopping till I got to Elsie's. Eddie was still sleeping, but he woke up while Elsie and I were talking and I gathered him up and took off, but not before he pointed a little finger at Elsie and said, "Doe."

I corrected him and tried to get him to say her name but about all I got was a hiss. But hearing the attempt, she was thrilled. And he had pulled himself up on his two feet a couple of times for her, so she was ecstatic at his progress.

The first thing I did when we got home was to call Jack to tell him about Bill Jamieson's stay at Trenton State, but Jack was off on a call so I had to leave a message, knowing he probably wouldn't get back to me in time for him to make a call to the prison.

Then I called Mel, who had just come home from school.

"Are you inviting me over or am I inviting you?" she said with her customary exuberance.

"I'm inviting you, just in case Jack gets back to the station house and gives me a call. I have something important to tell him."

"Chris, I can't believe it. You're doing it again. We'll be there in ten. I hope my sweetie is awake."

"Awake and doing new tricks."

"I can't waste time talking. Good-bye."

I laughed as I hung up. Not being the most outgoing person in the world, I have been grateful since I moved into this house that the luck of proximity gave me Mel as a neighbor. She does all kinds of things that I believe I can't do, and she does them with energy and enthusiasm and absolute perfection. She comes by it very honestly. I believe to this day that I would never have bought myself a wedding dress if it hadn't been for her mother. who took me under her wing and saw to it that everything was done and done right.

"Eddie," I said to my little son in his playpen, "Mel is coming. And Sari and Noah are coming, too. They're coming to see you."

He smiled as though what I had said made sense, and then he babbled and went back to his toys. As I went to unlock the door, I heard the Gross gang.

We hugged as she entered, and then I gave each of the children a hug and kiss as Mel went to the playpen to see Eddie.

"He's standing," she shrieked. "Chris, you didn't tell me. Eddie's standing." Mel lifted him up as I got there and gave him a million kisses, making him giggle.

We talked about his new accomplishments for a while and then got on to better things. Mel had brought brownies, baked yesterday ("It was Sunday and we weren't going anywhere"), so I boiled some water for tea, the two of us sitting in the kitchen, leaving the kids to themselves in the family room.

"How's teaching?" I asked.

"I have the most fabulous class. They are such darlings. I think this will be my best semester ever. They're bright and clever and they're just a pleasure. When do you go back?"

"Tomorrow morning. I'm really looking forward to it. Eddie loves Elsie and he won't miss me one long morning a week."

"And you'll get out and feel like a human being and use your brain and come back happy."

"You're right. I'm glad I didn't give it up. I was even thinking about taking on a second class next semester."

"You can't do that," Mel said with horror.

"Why not?"

"The American justice system will fall apart. Murders will go unsolved; criminals will go unjudged and unpunished." She looked so serious I was afraid to smile.

"This can't go on forever, Mel," I said reasonably.

"Why not? You've got yourself a nice little reputation and even if you don't stumble on bodies yourself, figuratively, if not literally, people will come to you. They already have. They're not going to stop."

"Mel, you are the original ego booster."

"No. I just speak the truth. Look, I'm sure you're a great teacher. I love hearing about your classes and your students. But you have other gifts and you must continue to use them. It's why you left the convent. Which reminds me, have you talked to Sister Joseph about all this?"

"She came out for twenty-four hectic but terrific hours, and we interviewed a bunch of people together."

"She must have loved that," Mel said. "Of course, I would love it, too, being right there in the center of the action, but it's not my calling. It's yours, friend."

"Oh Mel," I said, for at least the hundredth time, "what would I do without you?"

We shared the brownies with the children, not that we had a choice, and I gave Eddie a couple of crumbs that I'm sure made him feel that those awful mushy foods he got at mealtimes should be replaced, and we put aside a couple of squares for the love of my life, who would come home tired and hungry about six hours from now. And we talked.

"So," Mel said, "aside from a couple of murders, now was Fire Island and Uncle Max's house and the beach and all the rest of it?"

"Incomparable, luxurious, restful, an absolute pleasure. No wonder you look forward to it every summer. And how about your wedding in California?"

We traded stories as we had come to do as we became friends. Mel had done a fair amount of traveling in her life, something I had not, and I loved hearing about faraway places that we might one day visit, when the days of diapers and teething and strained foods were behind us. I didn't yearn to see those places; I just felt they were something to look forward to when time and money allowed.

"We even got to visit some wineries," Mel said, after telling some wedding tales. "You know how Hal enjoys his wines. I took over the driving at that point, just to be on the safe side."

"Well, it's good to be home and better to see you."

"Do you think you know who the killer is?"

"I don't, although I have a good suspect. I'm hoping that when Jack calls the prison, he'll get a list of people who were released on that date. Even if none of the names rings a bell, we'll have a rough age we can use to identify William Jamieson's real name. There ought to be a file on him with a hometown and maybe some family names. Maybe even a wife. There's no reason to believe he was single, even if that's what he told Sally Holland. He told her he'd been in prison because of what she called pilfering or shoplifting. I doubt whether that was true. I expect he was convicted of something much more serious. And she admitted he'd hit her on occasion. She said all men did that."

"Well, she's got that wrong," Mel said firmly. "Very wrong. I feel sorry for a woman who thinks that's part of life with a man."

"So do I. But I can tell you, she was very fond of him. You can hear it when she talks about him."

"Well, I hope you find the person who killed her daughter."

"So do I. He shouldn't be walking around a free man."

I knew before I answered the phone that it was too late for anything to be done today. Jack said, "I only have a second."

I knew he didn't want to be late for his first class of the semester. "I'll tell you later."

"OK." Click. And he was off.

"Later" was after ten that night. After two relaxing weeks, Jack looked totally undone by his first day back at work and at law school classes. Also very hungry. I was glad there were brownies to raise his spirits.

"Got called out this afternoon and the crime scene unit got stuck in traffic, and I thought I'd have to walk in late on my first class. Not something I look forward to."

"Did you make it?"

"Just."

"Tell me when it's OK to talk."

He gave me a smile. "Talk, honey. It's easier to listen."

"William Jamieson did time in Trenton State."

"Now that's talkin'. Go on."

"Sally Holland almost didn't tell me. But she knew the date he got out. It was Tina's birthday."

"Not bad. I really didn't think you'd get much out of her, or at least, not much that would be useful. I'll call the prison tomorrow and see what they come up with. How long ago did he get out?"

"Most likely eighteen years ago. She thought she could be off on the year but not on the date."

"They'll have to do a manual search. It's too long ago for the file to be on computer. I'll get a list of everyone who got out that day and we'll see who fits the description. He was in his twenties. That's about all we know about him. She didn't know his real name?"

"He never told her. She didn't know he was in prison till they became friends. She said he only told her because he trusted her. But she picked him up at a bus stop the day he got out of prison. So he was using the name Jamieson right from the beginning."

"Which means he had someone on the outside who arranged the new identity. Maybe got him a Social Security card and a driver's license. That's a good friend, or a wife or girlfriend."

"Or a dad." I handed him the letter.

"Buzzy. Look at that, no return address, no one referred to by name. They were being very careful." He put his fork down and finished reading the letter. "He could have maintained two separate identities for a while after he got out. For his new friends, for his employer, he was Bill Jamieson. But if he got out of Trenton State, he had to see a parole officer for some period of time. So for that, he used his real name. He goes to see the probation officer and the guy never knows there's a second identity. When Jamieson's clean, he chucks his old name completely."

"Sounds easy."

"It is when you've got help on the outside. He probably met the guy with the papers or picked them up at a post office box somewhere."

"Jack."

"What's up?"

"I just realized. Dodie Murchison didn't call." I was

suddenly feeling clammy. "She said she'd call tonight." I looked at my watch. "I wonder if she's all right."

"She didn't give you a number, did she?"

"Nothing. She said she'd call." I went to the phone and tried her home number. Nothing. I left a message on the machine and hung up. "I'll call her office tomorrow. I don't like this."

"I don't either, but there's nothing we can do. Her car's already in the alarms and if she has any sense, she's driving a friend's car or a rental."

"She asked me to talk to Sally Holland. She wouldn't forget to call and find out what happened."

"Someone could've followed you to Greenwillow last night."

"Mr. Hershey," I said. "My God. I hope she's all right."

27

I wasn't in the best shape Tuesday morning. Jack promised to call Trenton State as soon as he got to the station house, and to make sure that he got it done before he caught a case, he left a little early. I was ready early myself because I had to pack Eddie off to Elsie and get to the college in time to pick up my class list and all the tons of notices that were always in my box, instructions on everything from where to park to how to fill out the new, very necessary forms that appeared at the start of each new school year.

There had been no word from Dodie and I was scared. When I got to the college, I called her law firm and asked for her. I was told by a crisp young female voice that Ms. Murchison was on vacation and I was welcome to leave a message. I didn't.

Maybe it was nothing but I couldn't accept that. Dodie was no fool. She wanted to know who had killed Ken Buckley and Tina Frisch so that she would be off the hook. It was possible, as Jack suggested. that her disappearance was an indication that much that she had told me was false, that she, in fact, had killed both of them and that sending me on a wild goose chase had just given her another twenty-four hours to effect her disappearance.

The other possibility was, as Jack had also suggested, that someone had followed me—or Jack—on Sunday night to Greenwillow and had seen Dodie drive up, go in, and leave. And then he had followed her because, if she had been the last person to talk to Tina, she might know what Tina knew, who the killer of Ken Buckley was.

There was also the chance that she had been picked up somehow by the police, perhaps for speeding, and a check determined that she was wanted for questioning in a homicide case. If that had happened, having Tina's diamond earring in her purse wasn't going to help her case.

It was a good thing I had done all this before. I found my class assignment and my room, met all the new students and began to commit their names to memory. Some of them had the book, others didn't. Nothing new there. One thought this was an advanced class and left. Another found this wasn't the class she was assigned to, but she decided to stay and see whether she liked it. I even managed to get some teaching done when all the bookkeeping was taken care of.

When it was over, I dropped off my attendance list at the registrar and hurried to the cafeteria for a quick lunch. Then I drove home to see if Jack had called.

There was a message from him on the machine: "Talked to a guy at Trenton State just now. He'll get back to me later today with the list of names of people released on that date. Sorry I couldn't do anything sooner but you know how it is. I also called Chief Springer and asked if Dodie Murchison had been found. He said she hadn't turned up and he figures she's out of the country by now. Give me a call when you get home."

I called but he wasn't there, so I did my shopping before driving over to Elsie's to pick up Eddie. If any police department had arrested Dodie for any reason, her name would have come up on their computer as wanted in Suffolk County. So it was a pretty good bet that she was still at large—or being held somewhere by a killer.

All kinds of ideas were dancing in my head as I got Eddie out of the car and into the house. I put him safely in the playpen and then went back out for my bags of groceries. It took two trips and when I came inside for the last time, the phone was ringing. I literally dropped the bags and ran.

"Chris?" my husband's voice said.

"Just a little out of breath. What've you got?"

"The name we've been looking for."

"Tell me."

"Five men were released from Trenton State that day. Two were in their forties, one in his thirties, two in their twenties. A twenty-six-year-old was black, so I figured that was a long shot. The other guy—are you ready for this?"

"Ready. Tell me."

"The last guy was named Richard Springer, nickname Buzz or Buzzy."

"Oh, my God."

"Right. So our friend Curt Springer knew his brother had gone to Fire Island and was never heard of again and he got the police chief job in Blue Harbor a couple of years later, probably so he could investigate his brother's disappearance in his spare time. It also explains how Buzzy got out of prison with a new identity. A cop—and Curt was a cop somewhere or other before he got this job—would know exactly how to get him the papers he'd need to start a new life."

"Jack, I'm afraid he may have killed Dodie."

"OK, listen to me. I've just called the sheriff's office in Suffolk County. They're up to speed on the Buckley and Frisch homicides. I'm going to take the night off from my classes and go out to Blue Harbor and try to talk to Curt. He kind of liked me and maybe I can talk him into telling me where Dodie is. It's two days since you saw her. If he hasn't killed her, she may not last much longer."

"You can't take off the time from your classes, Jack," I said.

"This is life and death."

"I'll do it. I'll call Elsie to come right away. She can stay over if I don't get back in good time."

"Chris, I don't think that's such a—"

"Jack, if you miss the second night of classes—"

"OK, OK. I'll call the deputy back and let him know. But I don't like this."

I assured him I could handle it, more to hear myself say it than to tell him what he already knew. He gave me the name of the deputy and all the information I would need.

When I got off the phone, I called Elsie, who said she would come right over, and then Deputy Shrager, who said he would meet me at the ferry as soon as I could get there.

It would be up to me to coax Curt Springer into disclosing where Dodie Murchison was being held. If he had her, and she was still alive.

I had thrown a change of clothes into a small bag. I am a day person, not a night person, and I fade fast after dark, so I didn't look forward to driving home late at night. By the time I got to the Bay Shore ferry slip, it was close to six. It took no time to find Deputy Shrager; he had been looking out for me for half an hour.

"Thank you for coming, Mrs. Brooks," he said. "We've been looking everywhere we can think of that a person could be hidden, but we've come up with nothing. There's a ferry leaves here in about ten minutes. One of our people is already in Blue Harbor and we're in contact. Springer's in his office. Your husband's given us the whole story. We'd just like you to sweet-talk Springer, see if he'll tell you where the Murchison woman is. Tell him anything you want. We just want to find her alive. We want to make a case against Springer, but she's our first priority."

I said I would do my best. We got on the ferry with a handful of people. It would be a longer trip than usual. With the reduced number of passengers, two routes had been combined and Blue Harbor was the second stop.

We talked on the way. His name was Terence Shrager and he asked me to call him Terry. He was a lean man with the weather-beaten face of a farmer and a calm, reassuring demeanor. It didn't take an expert to see that I was nervous, but I relaxed some as we talked.

During the forty-minute run, he talked several times on a cell phone to the man already in Blue Harbor. "Springer's still there," Terry said, each time he got off. As we approached the pier with all the red wagons hanging from their hooks, he said, "Brad Schofield's waiting for us. He's going to walk you to Springer's office. Springer has never laid eyes on any of us and we've done our best to look like we belong."

I smiled. He was wearing a plain green T-shirt and jeans that were loose around the ankles so I knew that was where his weapon was holstered. The ferry came in smoothly, and we stepped off after a couple of men who looked as though they had just finished a day on Wall Street.

A man in cutoffs and a big sweatshirt moved toward us through the small group waiting with wagons, and was introduced to me as Brad Schofield. We started walking toward the Blue Harbor municipal building.

I left the door to the outer office open as we had agreed.

The secretary was gone. I went up to the closed door to the chief's office and knocked.

"Come in," Springer called.

I opened the door and walked inside, leaving the door open behind me. "Hi, Chief."

Springer looked surprised. "Mrs. Brooks. I thought you folks left the island on Sunday."

"We did. I came back to talk to you." I sat in the chair on the visitor's side of the desk.

"About what?"

"About Dodie Murchison. I'm very worried about her. I think you know where she is."

His eyes darted around before settling on me, as though he sensed that something was going on behind his back. Then he smiled. "How would I know? I told Jack when he called this morning she hasn't turned up anywhere. I'd put money on her being long gone, out of the country maybe."

"Curt," I said, using his first name for the first time, "we know what happened to Buzzy."

"You—" He stopped, looking confused. "What are you trying to tell me?"

"We know how your brother died. It was in the house that burned down fifteen years ago."

"I don't know what you're talking about." He had paled and I thought his hand was trembling.

"Richard Springer got out of Trenton State Prison about eighteen years ago. Someone had arranged a new name and a new identity for him. He became William Jamieson. He met a woman the day he got out of prison and he became friends with her. She had a little girl who was only five years old at that time. The little girl's name was Tina Frisch."

This time his hand shook visibly. "Tina Frisch knew him?"

"She thought he was her father," I said, "but he wasn't. She'd been looking for him for years. By coincidence she came out to Blue Harbor this summer, the same summer you found out what happened to your brother."

"Ken Buckley killed him."

"No, he didn't, Curt. A young girl killed him after he made advances. It was an accident. She was trying to protect herself. Ken Buckley just came in afterwards to clean up the mess."

"That's a lie. Buckley killed him and got rid of his body—I don't know how. They all covered up for him. Everybody here was his friend. They talk about the blue wall of silence. It's nothing compared to Blue Harbor."

I didn't want to argue about it. "Dodie Murchison was an innocent victim in all this. Please tell me where she is."

"I don't know. I've been looking for her since she left Fire Island."

"I saw her Sunday night."

"You saw her and you didn't report it?" He was doing his best to sound angry. "She's a suspect in two homicides."

"You followed us home from Bay Shore, didn't you? You followed us to the place where I met Dodie. And then you followed her when she left."

"You've got a good imagination, Mrs. Brooks. Murchison killed Tina Frisch. Her fingerprints are all over the bicycle, all over the gate. We've got a good case against her. I bet she even has the missing diamond earring."

I think that was the moment I became absolutely certain that he had her. He had gone through her handbag and found the earring. I wondered whether he had killed her and made it look like suicide. With the earring, he might even have a pretty good circumstantial case.

"Did you see it?" I asked.

"What?"

"The diamond earring."

"I didn't see anything. Look, Mrs. Brooks, you're a smart lady but you've got this all wrong. You're right, I had a brother. He was a good kid who made one mistake and he paid for it. Buckley killed him—maybe they got into a fight—and Buckley kept it a secret for fifteen years. I don't know who killed Buckley, maybe Murchison, maybe Tina Frisch, but he got what he deserved."

"I know you did it, Curt," I said, keeping my voice low and steady. "Jack knows you did it. It was a misunderstanding. You thought Ken killed your brother and you wanted to punish him, but Ken never killed anybody, and all Tina wanted was to find out what happened to a man she thought might be her father. The only thing I don't understand is why Ken had no clothes on when they found his body."

Something changed in him when I finished speaking. "You think I'm a fag, is that what you think?"

"I don't think anything. I just wondered—"

"I made him undress," Springer said, his face changing. "I wanted it to look like he was waiting for a woman, like a woman killed him. I used a woman's gun. He was a ladies' man, that son of a bitch. I figured he killed my brother over a woman."

"So you made him undress and get into bed. And then you shot him."

"Yeah. I let him know what for, too. And then I went downstairs and got the stove going and put some papers on it so they'd burn the place down."

"Like the Norrises' house."

"Just like the house where they burned my brother."

"Is that when Tina came in?"

"I don't know when she came in. It could've been while I was upstairs with Buckley. I found her in the living room just before I ducked out. She was scared, as if she knew what had happened upstairs. I told her if she ever said a word about what happened, I'd kill her."

"She never did say a word, not to me and not to anyone I know of. What happened then?"

"There was an old fireman's coat hanging on a hook. She grabbed it and put it over her head. Everything was burning by then and I could hear noise outside. I went out and made like I'd just got there. She just disappeared."

Through the crowd with the coat over her head, making her way to safety and anonymity until she bumped into me. "Why did you kill her, Curt?"

"I saw her with the woman lawyer. I figured she'd told her everything. I hid near the grouper house she was staying in and waited for her to come back. I got myself a goddamn tick, if you can believe it." He showed me a red mark on his forearm where he must have taken it out with a needle. That was his punishment for hiding in the tall grasses. "When the lawyer left, I grabbed Tina. And if it makes any difference, I didn't follow you to Bay Shore. I took an earlier ferry and waited for you."

So that was the story. He had probably never noticed that his second victim was wearing only one earring.

"Please," I said. "Please tell us where Dodie Murchison is."

"What's it worth to you?"

"Jack and I will do our best to help you. I have a wonderful lawyer friend and I'll ask him to defend you."

"Sure." He opened a drawer with his right hand and I got scared. I knew the deputies were in the building. With luck, they were in the secretary's office, just the other side of the open door behind me. Springer didn't ordinarily carry a gun but I knew he had one, and as the drawer slid open, I knew it must be there.

"Curt," I said.

He pulled a gun out of the drawer as I watched in

horror, said something that sounded like "Gibson," and as I screamed and dropped to the floor, there was a terrible explosion.

28

He had blown his brains out.

In the seconds after the shot, the deputies came running. I was on the floor, crying, my hands over my ears. They lifted me very tenderly and took me out, shielding my eyes so that I did not have to see what was on the other side of the desk. Terry Shrager made a bunch of phone calls as I sat, calming down, in the secretary's chair.

When I was able to speak, I said, "Did you hear what he said?"

They both said no.

"It sounded like 'Gibson.' Does that mean anything to you?"

Apparently it didn't. Terry made another phone call, this one sounding as though it was to a police department. After he identified himself, he said, "Who's Gibson?" He listened, shook his head, and closed up the phone.

"Maybe it's a town," I said.

They looked at each other. As sheriff's deputies, they would be familiar with the cities and towns of their county and probably of most of Long Island.

Brad Schofield picked up the phone on the secretary's desk as the first of the ambulance volunteers ran into the room. As Terry explained what had happened and as others followed with resuscitation equipment, Brad was asking someone at the other end of the line who Gibson might be.

He held for a few seconds, but before he got an answer, one of the paramedics called, as he ran, "It's a street in Bay Shore. There's a municipal parking lot there you can park in before you take the ferry."

Brad looked at all of us. "Springer, does he have a car or van he could have left there?"

"Give it a try," Terry said. "Call Patman."

They kept the line open as Patman drove from the ferry to wherever the lot was, not far because he arrived there in only a minute or two, his siren blaring.

"He's there," Schofield said. "He's checking out cars. There aren't many. Terry, see if you can find out if Springer has a car registered to him."

Terry was already on his cell phone doing just that. In the age of technology, lives can be saved by the speed of a computer. Terry called out a license plate number and Brad relayed it to Patman at the Gibson parking lot.

"Got it!" Brad sang out, sheer joy on his face.

I was near tears again, praying for Dodie's life. "Get an ambulance over there, OK?" I said, my voice shaking.

Terry got back on the cell phone as a woman, screaming, came nearer and nearer. Mrs. Springer. I had forgotten that Curt had a wife and family, that their lives had just been broken into little bits by a gunshot.

In she came, her hair flying, two men trying to stop her from entering the scene of her husband's suicide. I turned away.

"He's got her," Brad shouted from the telephone.

"Is she alive?" I whispered.

"Don't know. Hold on. Yeah, she's breathing. Not in good shape. I hear the siren. The ambulance is on its way."

I put my head down and cried.

* * *

I saw to it that I recovered quickly. Dodie was being taken to the nearest hospital, and I had been given a can of Coke to revive what was left of my spirits. We went next door to the firehouse where it was a little calmer, and somebody brought me something to eat.

"You can go back anytime you want. Chris," Terry said. "We're under control here. You did a great job."

I shook my head. "It isn't over," I said. "I need to know what they did with the body."

"What body?"

"The man who was killed accidentally fifteen years ago."

"Don't know what you're talkin' about."

"It's what started all this. He was Curt Springer's brother. He died of a knife wound and Ken Buckley covered it up by burning down the house the killing took place in."

Terry Shrager looked at me as though I were delusional. "I only know about the Buckley and Frisch homicides," he said. "What you're talking about, I don't know anything about it."

I rested my forehead in my hand, trying to think. The Hersheys might know but they'd never say anything. If Eve Buckley knew, she'd probably deny it. And then I remembered. "Chief La Coste," I said. "He told me the first time we talked at his house. He said, 'I know where all the bodies are buried.' That's what he meant." I stood.

"You feeling OK now?" Terry said anxiously.

"I'm fine. I need to walk to the ocean beach. There's someone I have to talk to."

"I'll go with you," Brad said.

We walked the width of the island, the street we were on eventually becoming a pathway onto the dune. I pulled my sandals off and walked down onto the beach in bare feet, remembering the blissful two weeks Jack and Eddie and I had shared, what seemed a lifetime ago.

It was already dark and Brad asked if I needed a flashlight.

"No thanks. He's easy to spot." We walked toward the Margulies's house. The Chief would be in his usual spot before we got that far. I kept my eyes on the dune and finally, there it was, the glow of a cigarette, a shadow in a sitting position.

"Hi, Chief," I called.

"Who's that?"

"Chris Brooks."

"Chris. What're you doin' here? I thought you went back home already."

"Came back to ask you a question." I told Brad to stay behind and I climbed the dune to where he sat in his lightweight chair.

"All the way back from wherever, just to ask me a question?"

"It's an important one."

"OK. Shoot."

"It's about the Great Fire, Chief. I know all about it, about the body in the kitchen." I stopped, but he didn't say anything, just looked at me. "I found out yesterday who he was."

"You don't say."

"You told me last week—it seems like a year ago but it was only last week—you told me you knew where all the bodies were buried. Where's that one buried?"

He blew smoke and smiled. "In the park." He pointed to the left, toward England and France and the wilderness area at the eastern end of the island.

"Right here on Fire Island?"

"Right here."

"But there are animals. Wouldn't they dig up—?"

"Deer," he said. "They're vegetarians, deer are. They stay away from the smell of blood."

"I see. But how—?" And then I saw it. "You used the fireboat, didn't you?"

"Why not? Even the old one was big enough for a couple of men and what was left of another in a body bag. We pulled it on a wagon to the bay to where the boat was anchored. Wasn't easy but we got it there. Ken and me, we did it in the middle of the night."

"Can you show us where you buried him?"

"I could do that. But not at night. I made that trip one time at night. That was enough for a lifetime, even a long one."

"Ken Buckley called you that night?"

"Sure did. Told me what happened. Said the man was a stranger, nobody knew who. When Tina came to me in July, I knew we hadn't buried him deep enough. You say you know who he was?"

"Curt Springer's brother."

"My God in heaven." He put out what was left of his cigarette, bending to snuff it in the sand.

"Can I walk you home, Chief?"

"I think I'll just sit here awhile and do some thinkin'. They gonna ask me to take them to the body?"

"Probably."

"Hope it's a bigger boat this time."

"I'm sure it will be."

29

I insisted that they take me to the hospital where Dodie had been taken, and I got to see her for a minute. She looked wasted and half-dead but she was at least half-alive, and she held my hand and even managed to squeeze it. She was dehydrated, among other problems, but the doctor I talked to sounded optimistic.

Terry Shrager and Brad Schofield refused to let me drive home alone, even though it meant hours there and back for them. Terry drove my car and Brad followed in his. It was a long drive and when we got home, they came inside and met Jack and stayed for coffee.

Jack was beside himself that he had let me go to see Springer alone but I told him, truthfully, that missing the second night of classes would have started him off all wrong in his law school semester. I guess I know how I feel when people miss a class early on and come back with unbelievable excuses. Jack's a cop so his excuses probably have a more plausible ring, but you never know how your professor feels and it's crazy to take a chance. At least, that's how I feel.

Dodie Murchison recovered, thank God, and got back to work in a couple of weeks. Eventually, the diamond earring found its way back to Sally Holland, along with the one Tina was wearing when Springer broke her neck. We never learned what Springer was planning to do with Dodie, but it didn't matter.

The Blue Harbor governing board decided unanimously to abolish the position of police chief and to rely entirely on the Suffolk County Sheriff's Department. Mrs. Springer sold the restaurant to an entrepreneurial chef who already had one restaurant on Long Island and promised to make the one in Blue Harbor a gourmet affair that would bring people across the bay just for dinner.

Max Margulies, who had never met us, invited us to his home, along with Melanie and Hal, later in September, for dinner and a rundown of what had really happened. Jack and I had decided not to say what we knew about the killing of Richard Springer unless we were asked by police or sheriff's department, and they never did. What Jack knew was hearsay anyway, since I had done all the questioning and had heard all the answers. I can't say that I'm happy about the Hersheys' daughter plunging a knife into a man's chest, but I assume the reason I heard from Dodie who heard it from Ken Buckley who heard it from—oh well, you get the picture.

When Dodie was feeling up to it, she invited Jack and me to dinner at the most expensive restaurant I had ever been to. Looking at the menu made my stomach do flip-flops, and I think she sensed it, reassuring me that this was quite affordable. We began the evening at her Manhattan apartment, a beautiful home on a high floor with views of the George Washington Bridge, the Hudson River, and even the Statue of Liberty on a clear day or night. And of course, the sunset, since it faced west. A nice perk for a lady who deserved it.

* * *

The remains of Richard Springer were recovered soon after the night I talked to Chief La Coste. He guided the sheriff over to the place where he and Ken Buckley had buried the body bag just over fifteen years earlier. An autopsy was inconclusive, but the medical examiner thought there was a good chance the person had died of a knife wound. It wasn't hard to find the dead man's family once it was established that he was Curt Springer's brother.

There was still one unanswered question, the hug. Why had Eve Buckley hugged Tina Frisch that morning outside the grouper house? I waited a long time to find out. Eventually, I called Mary Ellen Tyler and she got back to me a few days later.

Eve scarcely remembered it when she was asked. But as she and her sister talked, she remembered that Tina had been so sympathetic, so sweet, so emphatic that she had not been anywhere near the Buckley home the day of the fire, that when Eve said good-bye to her, it seemed appropriate to give her a hug.

I don't know if we'll ever visit Fire Island again. Maybe Mel's Uncle Max will invite us for another vacation. Maybe we'll rent a house for a couple of weeks one summer. Maybe we'll just hang onto the memory and let it lie.

I suppose I will never see Chief La Coste again. But I think of him from time to time. I've written him a couple of notes and I put his name on my Christmas card list. What I'm certain of is that I'll remember that shadow on the dune, that glow of light, that remarkable memory of his for the rest of my life. And once in a while I'll wonder what other secrets remain in that old head. After all, he said he knew where all the bodies were buried. Plural. Was it a turn of phrase or a statement of fact? I guess I'll never know.

Even after leaving the cloistered world
of St. Stephen's Convent for suburban
New York State, Christine Bennett still finds
time to celebrate the holy days.

Unfortunately, in the secular world
the holidays seem to end in murder—
and it's up to this ex-nun to discover
who commits these unholy acts.

LEE HARRIS

The Christine Bennett Mysteries

Published by Fawcett Books.
Available in your local bookstore.